*Monsieur Pamplemousse and
the French Solution*

*Monsieur Pamplemousse and
the French Solution*

MICHAEL BOND

First published in Great Britain in 2007 by
Allison & Busby Limited
13 Charlotte Mews
London W1T 4EJ
www.allisonandbusby.com

A CIP catalogue record for this book is available from
the British Library.

10 9 8 7 6 5 4 3 2 1

13-ISBN 978-0-7490-8022-8

Typeset in 11/16 pt Sabon by
Terry Shannon

Printed and bound in Great Britain by
MPG Books Ltd, Bodmin, Cornwall

MICHAEL BOND was born in Newbury, Berkshire in 1926 and started writing whilst serving in the army during the Second World War. In 1958 the first book featuring his most famous creation, Paddington Bear, was published and many stories of his adventures followed. In 1983 he turned his hand to adult fiction and the detective cum gastronome par excellence Monsieur Pamplemousse was born. This is the sixteenth book to feature Monsieur Pamplemousse and his faithful bloodhound Pommes Frites. Michael Bond was awarded the OBE in 1997. He is married, with two grown-up children, and lives in London.

CHAPTER ONE

'*Merde!*'

The moment Monsieur Pamplemousse placed his ID card against a brass plate set in the wall outside *Le Guide*'s headquarters and nothing happened, he knew it was going to be 'one of those days'.

By rights, there should have been a discreet buzz, followed by a faint click as a small oak door let into one of a much larger pair swung open on its well-oiled hinges, thus allowing free passage to any member of staff wishing to enter the august premises on foot. Instead of which...what happened? Nothing!

He tried repeating the process, this time holding the card in place rather longer than before, but again to no avail.

Looking, if possible, even more upset than his master, Pommes Frites lowered himself gently onto the cold pavement, stared at the offending piece of metal as though daring it to misbehave for a third time, then raised his head and gave vent to a loud howl.

To anyone close by, the mournful tone would have said it

all, but it was lunchtime and the rue Fabert was deserted. That being so, and having decided knocking on the door would be a waste of both time and knuckles, Monsieur Pamplemousse applied a shoulder to it.

For all the effect it had, he might have been paying a surprise visit to Fort Knox with a view to enquiring how things were going with their gold reserves. There was what the powers that be might have called a negative response.

Nursing his right shoulder, the very same shoulder that had performed yeoman service whenever called upon to act as a battering ram during his years with the Paris Sûreté, he had to admit he found the situation extremely annoying.

He wouldn't have minded quite so much had he not received a message from the Director summoning him back to headquarters *tout de suite*.

His first thought had been 'Not again!' followed in quick succession by 'What is it this time?' and 'If it's *that* important, why isn't he using the word "*Estragon*"; *Le Guide*'s standard code word for use in an emergency?'

He had spent most of the journey turning it over in his mind. The last time he had received such a summons had been when they were called in to offer advice on a possible terrorist attack on the food chain. It had all been very Hush Hush.

Once again, no reason had been given, but by comparison, the latest message – DROP EVERYTHING. PLEASE RETURN TO BASE IMMEDIATELY – was positively verbose. Although it imparted a sense of urgency, the use of the word 'Please' – not a word that normally figured large in Monsieur Leclercq's vocabulary – was unusual to say the least. It struck a personal note.

It was not as though he had wasted any time getting there.

Setting off from Rodez in the Midi-Pyrénées at a ridiculously early hour, he had driven the 600 kilometres to Paris almost non-stop. He hadn't even been home, but instead headed straight for the office.

To arrive and find they were locked out was akin to arriving at a theatre all set for an evening's entertainment, only to discover it was the wrong night. Both were equally dispiriting.

An even more frustrating aspect of the whole affair was that it had meant cutting short his current tour of duty. On the principle of saving the best until last, he had been looking forward to rounding it off in the small town of Laguiole, home to both the eponymous cutlery firm and the equally renowned restaurant Bras, famous for the patron's wondrous ways with the flora of the region.

Anticipating a brief stop at the former to do some Christmas shopping for his wife, he had pictured heading up the Puech du Suquet, a small mountain just outside the town, arriving at the futuristic restaurant perched like a space capsule on its launch pad at the very top, in good time for lunch.

Overlooking the vast Aubrac plateau, there was very little in the way of natural growth that didn't find its way into Monsieur Bras's kitchen sooner or later. Wild herbs, fennel, sorrel, celeriac, coriander, garlic, all were grist to his mill.

It was the kind of gastronomic experience that made the time spent away from home, driving for hours on end and putting up in strange hotels, abundantly worthwhile.

Given that it was near the end of October and the hotel and its restaurant would soon be closing down for the winter months, the chance wouldn't come his way again until next March at the earliest, if then.

In all probability, anonymity being one of the keywords of *Le Guide*, he would find himself assigned to a very different part of France. Word travelled fast and it didn't do to become too well known in any one area.

His Cupillard Rième watch showed almost 12.45. Even now he might be tucking in to what Michel Bras called his *Gargouillou* – a warm salad of over twenty young vegetables, each separately steamed before being brought together in total harmony. The ingredients varied with the season of course, and no two days were alike, but they were always as fresh as they could possibly be. However, there was no point in dwelling on it.

He stared the massive oak doors. What now? He couldn't even make use of his mobile phone. The battery had gone flat halfway through his tour and he had left his charger at home.

Security at *Le Guide*'s offices in the 16th *arrondissement* of Paris was a serious matter at the best of times, but especially so during the latter part of the year. Staff were almost wholly engaged in the mammoth task of collating reports and information concerning some ten thousand or so hotels and restaurants across the length and breadth of *le hexagon*; afterwards checking and rechecking, first the galleys, then the page proofs and finally the guide itself.

In the months leading up to spring publication, secrecy was paramount. Anyone caught breaking the rule ran the risk of instant dismissal.

All the same, totally denying him entry seemed to be carrying things a little too far.

Wondering if, as occasionally happened with plastic cards, continuous use, or even long periods spent in juxtaposition with each other, had brought about a failure of the magnetic strip, he was about to reach for his handkerchief in the forlorn hope that a quick rub might do the trick when, to his surprise, the door in front of him swung open.

Pommes Frites immediately froze as they found themselves confronted by a man in uniform; a uniform, moreover, emblazoned with an alien emblem: BRINKS, a well-known security company. To complete the picture, he was wearing the kind of reflective sunglasses beloved of American traffic police.

'Looking for something, bud?'

'*Oui*,' replied Monsieur Pamplemousse.

'Business?'

Monsieur Pamplemousse held up his card. 'I happen to work here.'

The man reached out and took it from him.

'Ident?'

'Pamplemousse.' Given that his name was clearly embossed in thick black letters alongside his photograph, it seemed a somewhat pointless exercise. He was hardly likely to risk making up a false one.

'Grapefruit, huh?'

He felt rather than saw the other's eyes boring into his as comparisons between the image on the card and the real thing were made. For a brief moment, as the man held it up to the light, turning it first one way and then another, Monsieur Pamplemousse derived a certain vicarious pleasure in picturing a holographic effect coming into play. Ideally, in his mind's eye it would be the sticking out of a tongue. However, no such luck.

The man's face remained utterly impassive as he turned away, withdrew a mobile from his hip pocket and held a brief conversation.

'OK this time,' he said, grudgingly holding the door open. 'But you better go get an update on your card. It needs eyeball identification installed. You can get it done in back of reception.'

Feeling his hackles rise, Monsieur Pamplemousse stared at his reflection in the man's sunglasses for a full ten seconds, long enough for his eyeballs to be permanently embedded in the other's memory. Comparisons with attempting to enter Fort Knox were clearly not so wide of the mark after all.

Signalling Pommes Frites to follow on, he retrieved his card and passed through the opening, wondering as he did so if his friend and mentor would receive similar treatment. One glance was sufficient. Pommes Frites' tail was standing bolt upright – a warning sign if ever there was one, and it proved more than sufficient.

Monsieur Pamplemousse thought he detected the security guard mouthing the words *trottoir royale*.

At least, despite the phoney American accent and the glasses, it meant he was sufficiently well versed in the French language to know the slang phrase for mongrel. He hoped for the man's sake his friend and mentor hadn't registered it. He was sensitive to such things.

Fearing the worst, he glanced back over his shoulder.

Normally the most docile of creatures, Pommes Frites was rooted to the spot, staring up the guard as though daring him to make a move.

Rather than call out, Monsieur Pamplemousse gave a brief whistle through his teeth and immediately regretted it as a series of high-pitched bleeps came from inside one of his jacket pockets.

The man from BRINKS heard it too and beckoned. 'Hey, you...let me see that.'

Noting the other's hesitation, he added: 'You wanna go on in or don't you?'

With a show of reluctance, Monsieur Pamplemousse retraced his steps, feeling inside the pocket for the offending object attached to his keyring. It went against the grain to afford the man any kind of pleasure, on the other hand he wouldn't be sorry to see the back of it.

A birthday present from Pommes Frites, it had turned out to be more trouble than it was worth, reacting as it did to all manner of sounds: ice cubes being emptied into a glass before going to bed at night, the playing of accordions on the Metro, and on one never to be forgotten occasion, during a violin solo at a concert. He still went hot and cold at the thought. Squeaking doors were another hazard; the oven door in their own apartment never failed to trigger it off. Doucette was always complaing about it.

It seemed a golden opportunity; one too good to miss.

The guard held out his hand. 'Gimme.'

'You are absolutely right,' said Monsieur Pamplemousse. 'I congratulate you on your powers of observation.'

Wondering if he hadn't perhaps laid it on a bit too thick, he was about to remove the alarm when he heard a deep-throated rumble from somewhere nearby. Looking down, he realised it was coming from Pommes Frites His top lip had somehow curled itself upwards into the distinct shape of a letter S, revealing a row of incisors, snow-white and razor sharp from much gnawing of bones over the years.

'Are you sure you want it?' he asked.

'Forget it!' With a show of considerable ill grace, the

security guard turned on his heels, unlocked the door to the tiny office just inside the gate, and disappeared from view, slamming it shut behind him.

Old Rambaud, the gatekeeper, must either be ill or on leave, for he was nowhere to be seen. Perhaps the new man was a temporary replacement.

Monsieur Pamplemousse sincerely hoped so. Looking at the state of Rambaud's window box, the sooner he came back to work the better.

The second thing that struck him as he led the way across the inner courtyard was that the fountain in the middle wasn't working. Apart from the annual spring clean, the only occasion he could remember that happening was when some joker introduced a piranha fish to the pool, nearly frightening a young secretary to death one lunchtime when she dangled a hand in the water while eating her sandwiches.

The next thing to catch his attention was the fact that the Director's top of the range black Citroën was missing from its normal parking place outside the private entrance to his quarters. In its place, occupying about a tenth of the space, short, squat and looking for all the world like a child's toy, stood a tiny Smart car.

It was something else unheard of. The Director's parking space was sacrosanct. No other member of staff would normally dare to make use of it.

Unless...he dismissed the thought. Even if the Director was on one of his periodic economy drives, it was inconceivable that the car belonged to him. The Citroën was his pride and joy; a status symbol, it would be the last thing to go. The Smart car wasn't even properly positioned.

Monsieur Leclercq was a stickler for things being in their correct place, particularly when it came to parking.

As he drew near, he also registered the fact that someone had sprayed the words PUTAIN PÉAGE in black paint across the car's rear window. Protesting against autoroute charges was one thing, but there was no excuse for spraying such a crudely impractical message on another person's car. It was an act of sheer vandalism.

Quickening his pace, he headed up the steps leading to the main entrance, steadying the plate-glass revolving doors momentarily with one hand in case Pommes Frites' tail, now waving to and fro in anticipation of better times ahead, jammed the mechanism as they passed through.

There was an unfamiliar girl on duty in reception and her greeting struck him as being perfunctory to say the least. She seemed to be making a point of *not* asking to see his pass. The question of registering his eyeballs didn't arise.

That again, was unusual. In Monsieur Leclercq's book, the first person a visitor came into contact with, whether by phone or in the flesh, was often the one who left a lasting impression. Staff were expected to behave accordingly.

Hesitating by the row of lifts, none of which happened to be at ground level, he decided to use the stairs instead, partly because he felt stiff after the long drive, but also to give himself time to marshal his thoughts.

To say the air was awash with undercurrents was putting it mildly. There was a feeling of anarchy in the air. If the inscription on the back of the car was anything to go by, it was no wonder security had been tightened.

But there again, it struck him there was something odd about the uniformed man on duty at the entrance; something about him that didn't ring true. Pommes Frites had certainly noticed it too.

Pausing on the third floor for a breather, Monsieur Pamplemousse decided it wouldn't do any harm to go through his IN tray and bring himself up to date before going on up to the Director's office. With that end in view he made his way along the corridor leading to the inspectors' room.

Expecting it to be empty, he was surprised to find several of his colleagues hard at work.

'If you're thinking of making out your expense sheets,' said Glandier, after the usual greetings had been exchanged, 'forget it. Madame Grante's on strike. P39's are piling up.'

'What? You're joking!'

'Well, she isn't in, and if she isn't on strike, I wouldn't lay any bets on her coming back.' Guilot, red-faced as ever from a continuing intake of carrot juice before meals, his preferred panacea for the occupational hazard of chronic indigestion, glanced up from a desk by the window. 'Can't say I blame her. Rumour has it the Director's been talking of replacing her with a laptop.'

'That's all very well,' said Glandier, 'but these things add up. Three months on the road costs a bomb. My bank account is suffering withdrawal symptoms.'

'If we don't get our expenses,' said Truffert, 'the job won't be worth a candle. If I'd realised what it was going to be like spending so much time eating on my own, I would have become a monk instead. The food may not always be as good, but at least you've got company.'

'Try telling that to a Trappist,' said Guilot. 'You wouldn't last long. At least we don't suffer a vow of silence.'

'I tell you something else,' Loudier broke in gloomily. 'If

Madame Grante doesn't come back soon, it's only a short step to outsourcing the whole of the Accounts Department to India.'

Listening to the others talk, Monsieur Pamplemousse began to feel it was a good thing he hadn't made it to Michel Bras after all.

'"Outsourcing" is the latest keyword,' explained Truffert. 'According to the grape vine there's a distinct possibility of doing the same thing with the canteen.'

'Not to India as well I hope,' said Monsieur Pamplemousse.

'At least the curry would be hot,' said Loudier. 'Even when it's cold, if you see what I mean.'

'Pommes Frites won't take kindly to it, that's for sure,' said Truffert. 'He'll be bringing his own if that happens. I can't see him missing out on Tuesday's *cassoulet*.'

'Think of the alternative,' persisted Loudier. 'Can you imagine…the staff of France's premiere food guide reduced to eating microwaved quiche Lorraine off plastic trays.'

'It's either that or portion control,' said Glandier. 'Take your pick.'

'You know what that means,' said Loudier. 'Less all round. You don't have portion control when people can have as much as they like.'

'It's like the old Woody Allen joke,' said Glandier. 'Not only is the food terrible, but it comes in such small portions.'

'When did all this come about?' asked Monsieur Pamplemousse.

'Over the last couple of weeks,' said Guilot.

'Who hasn't been phoning in?' asked Truffert pointedly.

Monsieur Pamplemousse had to admit he had been unusually lax in that respect.

Mobile phones had their uses, but losing the use of his own had felt like a luxury and he had made the most of it, especially while meandering across the Auvergne, where communication wasn't exactly on the cutting edge of technology at the best of times. It had been blissful.

'Monsieur Leclercq is allowing all this to happen?'

'That's the odd thing,' said Truffert. 'Ever since he arrived back from the States he's been a different person. Locking himself away with some high-flying time and motion consultant for hours on end; refusing to see anyone else.'

'If you want my opinion,' said Loudier, 'he's flipped. It's bad enough trying to get into the place as it is. As for eyeball recognition...they'll be installing passport control next. I shan't be sorry to say *adieu* to it all.'

Loudier had been coming up for retirement for as long as Monsieur Pamplemousse could remember. He had stayed on through a series of short-term contracts, but he sounded in earnest this time.

'You know what the next item on the agenda will be? VipChips! Have one implanted in your arm and you get keyless entry just by waving it at the lock.'

'That's not the only thing they can do,' said Truffert. 'In Africa they use them to keep track of wild animals. Mark my words...they'll end up being able to keep tabs on your comings and goings via a satellite. Think of that!'

'Talking of which,' said Loudier, 'has anyone heard from Madame Grante? I tried ringing the entry bell on her apartment in the rue des Renaudes, but there was no answer. To all intents and purposes she seems to have vanished off the face of the earth.'

'That's what comes of bringing in outsiders,' said Glandier. 'The founder must be turning in his grave. They didn't have business efficiency experts in his day. Can you imagine?'

'Péage by name,' said Loudier gloomily. 'Péage by nature.'

Monsieur Pamplemousse pricked up his ears. He wondered if it had anything to do with the graffiti on the back of the car.

'It isn't the first time it's happened,' explained Loudier. 'That honour goes to Monsieur Leclercq's car. It's at the dealers being attended to. Meantime his space is being used by our new business efficiency guru.'

'What's the betting the name was changed for the job?' said Guilot. 'It probably sounds better.'

'Very Hollywood,' said Glandier. 'Like Fred Astaire started out as Frederick Austerlitz.'

Having been brought up in the Savoy region where there wasn't much else to do during the winter months, Glandier was a dedicated cineaste and seldom let pass an opportunity to air his knowledge.

'And Doris Day was born Doris von Kappelhoff,' said Loudier.

'That's nothing.' Glandier sounded slightly piqued. 'Kirk Douglas began life as Iussur Danielovitch Demsky.'

'That sounds a pretty good reason for changing it,' said Guilot. 'Think of the trouble he would have had signing autographs if he hadn't.'

'I'll tell you something for nothing,' broke in Loudier. 'I looked Peáge up in the Paris phone book and there isn't single one listed.'

'Perhaps it started off as Plage,' said Guilot. 'It doesn't have to be major, one letter is often enough. People are always doing it with their kids. Adding a letter on, even simply taking one away. Then they have to go through life spelling it out.'

'There are laws in France about that kind of thing,' said Loudier.

'It happens,' said Monsieur Pamplemousse.

He was reminded of the time he'd had cause to investigate the Director's family plot in the Père Lachaise cemetery.

Monsieur Leclercq's family name was Leclerc. He must have decided at some point there were too many listed, so he'd added a 'q' to set himself apart. Knowing it was probably a sensitive point, Monsieur Pamplemousse decided not to mention the fact. It would create too much of a diversion.

His spirits sank still further as the conversation returned to the subject in hand: the future of *Le Guide*. Clearly, things were even worse than he had anticipated. He wondered if he should mention the summons he had received to return to headquarters, but decided to hold back for the time being, at least until he knew more about what was going on.

Leafing through the small pile of papers that had accumulated in his tray while he was away, Monsieur Pamplemousse reached for his pen...

'*Zut alors!*' He could have sworn he had it with him when they checked out of the hotel that morning.

'Here...use this.' Glandier tossed a Biro across the table.

Monsieur Pamplemousse eyed the object. Compared to his Cross writing instrument it didn't have the right feel at all, but beggars couldn't be choosers.

Initialing the first few papers, he made his excuses and continued on his way up to the Director's office on the 7th floor.

Hoping to catch Monsieur Leclercq's secretary for long enough to get the low-down, he was disappointed to find

Véronique emerging from the inner sanctum just as he entered the outer office.

She looked as though she had been crying, and her whispered '*bonne chance*' as she squeezed past struck him as being not so much a casual pleasantry as a heartfelt expression of some inner anguish.

Expecting to find the Director seated in the usual chair behind his desk, he was surprised to see it was empty.

Glancing round the room, he noted a small workstation in one corner; a laptop, mobile phone and desk-lamp neatly arranged on top, a plush office chair pushed into the kneehole. He assumed it must belong to the new adviser. It all looked very efficient.

A pair of sliding glass doors in the vast picture window were open, and despite the chill air, the Director was outside on the balcony encircling the whole of the mansard floor.

He appeared to be gazing into the middle distance, and it wasn't until Monsieur Pamplemousse and Pommes Frites drew near that he became aware of their presence and turned to face them.

It was several weeks since Monsieur Pamplemousse had last seen him, but during that time he appeared to have lost weight, visibly ageing in the process. He was also wearing dark glasses. It must be catching. No wonder Véronique looked worried.

'Ah, Pamplemousse!' he exclaimed. 'At long last. I have been looking out for you.'

Monsieur Pamplemousse resisted the temptation to say they would have arrived a quarter of an hour ago if they hadn't been locked out.

'We came as speedily as we could, monsieur.'

'I suppose the traffic was bad?' said Monsieur Leclercq.

'Not when we left,' said Monsieur Pamplemousse. 'There wasn't a car to be seen on the road at 5.30 this morning.'

'And you drove straight here?'

'We had a brief break stop at the Aire la Briganderie south of Orleans for Pommes Frites' benefit…'

'So that he could stretch his legs, I presume?'

'It was more urgent than that,' said Monsieur Pamplemousse loyally. 'He was badly in need of a *pipi*. As it was he only just made the silver birches in time. I also wanted to see if they had any string…'

'String!' boomed the Director.

'The passenger door had developed a rattle,' said Monsieur Pamplemousse. 'I was worried in case Pommes Frites fell out when we were cornering at speed.'

Monsieur Leclercq emitted a sigh. 'Ah, Aristide, I do wish you would pension off that old 2CV of yours and use a company car instead. Although, in the circumstances…' He broke off, dismissing whatever it was he had been about to say and instead glanced nervously at his watch.

Waving towards the visitor's chair, he followed them back into the room.

Pressing a button to trigger off the automatic closing of the sliding doors, there was a faint, but luxurious hiss of escaping air from his black leather armchair as he seated himself.

Leaning forward, he placed his elbows on the desk in front of him, forming a steeple with his hands as he gathered his thoughts.

It may have been the result of wearing dark glasses, but it struck Monsieur Pamplemousse that the overall effect was more suggestive of the Leaning Tower of Pisa than the upright spire of Sainte-Chapelle.

Happening to glance to his left during the pause that followed, he saw the door to the drinks cupboard was open. A bottle of Monsieur Leclercq's favourite cognac, Roullet Très Hors d'Age, was standing alongside an empty glass, and he couldn't help wondering if it were a case of cause and effect.

Also, it might have been his imagination or simply a trick of the light, but the heavily framed portrait above the cupboard appeared to show the sitter looking even more forbidding than usual. On second thoughts 'strained' might be a better description.

Perhaps Glandier was right and even now *Le Guide's* founder, Monsieur Hippolyte Duval, was in the process of turning over in his grave.

In much the same way that the subject's eyes in many portraits had a disconcerting habit of appearing to follow the viewer round a room, so the founder's portrait never failed to reflect the prevailing mood; his steely eyes acting like the mercury in a barometer as they moved up and down according to the prevailing temperature.

Monsieur Pamplemousse couldn't help but glance surreptitiously at his own watch. The hands showed 13.45.

Following whatever was on the menu for the main course at Michel Bras, poached *fois gras* with beetroot perhaps, or his renowned filet of Aubrac beef, they might have been rounding things off with a chocolate *coolant*: another 'signature' dish, inspired, so it was said, by a family skiing holiday. The warmth of a hollowed-out sponge, sometimes filled with fruit, at other times with chocolate or caramel, the whole capped with a scoop of frozen double cream, was intended to give the effect of a snow-covered mountain peak.

As he remembered it, the latter truly was the icing on the cake; much imitated, but never surpassed. It was no wonder the restaurant boasted three Stock Pots in *Le Guide*.

The thought reminded him of how hungry he felt, and he knew someone else who would be even more upset if he knew what was passing through his mind.

Except the 'someone else' in question, blissfully unaware of his master's thought processes, was making full use of the lull in order to look for the water bowl that was invariably made ready for him whenever he visited the Director's office. He peered round the desk and behind the waste bin, but he couldn't see it anywhere. Such a thing had never happened before, bringing home to him, as nothing else could, the full seriousness of the situation.

Having drawn a blank, he gave vent to a deep sigh and settled down at his master's feet to await developments.

The Director gave a start and came back down to earth from wherever he had been.

'No doubt, Pamplemousse,' he said, 'you are wondering why I sent for you.'

Monsieur Pamplemousse sat back in his chair. He couldn't have put it better if he tried.

'As you may know,' continued Monsieur Leclercq, 'I have recently returned from a visit to New York. While I was there, I paid a courtesy call on a company not dissimilar in size to our own.

'One of the things I discovered was that they have what they call a "vibe" manager; a person whose sole function it is to report back to the management on matters concerning staff satisfaction.

'In my position, Aristide, it is all too easy to lose touch with the rank and file.'

You're telling me, thought Monsieur Pamplemousse. Getting in touch with them from the beginning and staying that way might be the answer.

'Tell me, Aristide,' said Monsieur Leclercq, 'you are a man of the world, and I place great value on your powers of observation. How would you rate the vibes within our own organisation?'

Monsieur Pamplemousse hardly knew where to begin. 'I, too, have been away,' he said, slowly gathering his thoughts. 'But in the short time I have been back I have noticed a number of things. There is a feeling of unhappiness in the air. Rumours are rife, and since they are spreading in all directions, much as tiny waves are set in motion when you throw a stone into the waters of a lake, they are hard to evaluate.

'To put it bluntly, monsieur, I would say our own vibes indicate that matters have possibly reached an all-time low.'

'Ah!' Monsieur Leclercq shrank back in his seat. As he did so, there was another hiss of escaping air; almost as though he was being engulfed by the weight of some vast, overpowering tidal wave and had given up the fight. 'I feared as much.'

'Can I get you anything, monsieur?' Monsieur Pamplemousse voiced his fears as he jumped to his feet. 'A glass of cognac, perhaps?'

'You are a good man, Pamplemousse.' The Director reached for a handkerchief and dabbed at his forehead. 'Perhaps you would care to join me? I think you may be in need of one too when you hear what I have to tell you.'

An innocent enough remark: it seemed like a good idea to Monsieur Pamplemousse at the time.

Afterwards he was to realise that even a spider's web has to start somewhere.

CHAPTER TWO

'Life, Aristide,' began the Director, 'is not all champagne and boules.'

'That is true the world over,' said Monsieur Pamplemousse, doing his best to offer words of comfort. '*Par exemple*, I imagine in Russia they probably use the phrase "vodka and onions".'

'Onions?' repeated Monsieur Leclercq.

'I was thinking of those domes they have on top of their buildings,' said Monsieur Pamplemousse.

'In Grande Bretagne,' he continued, warming to his theme, 'I believe they say life is not all beer and skittles.'

'From what one reads of their behaviour at football matches, Pamplemousse,' said the Director testily, 'one could be forgiven for thinking it was. The perfidious Albions are past masters at the art of twisting facts to suit themselves.'

'I believe they feel the same way about us,' said Monsieur Pamplemousse. '*Vive la différence.*'

Monsieur Leclercq removed the dark glasses and leant back in his chair, gazing at the ceiling as though involved in a life and death struggle with his innermost thoughts.

'You were about to explain why we were summoned,' ventured Monsieur Pamplemousse.

The Director looked as though he was beginning to wish he hadn't.

'Perhaps,' he said, 'I should begin at the beginning.'

'It is always a good place,' said Monsieur Pamplemousse.

Recalling his long past visit to Père Lachaise, he couldn't help adding: 'Especially given your family motto – *Ab ovo usque ad mala.*'

The Director gave a start. '"From beginning to end". Your memory does you credit, Aristide. Although I fear the latter part of it is none too apposite at this juncture. The end is far from in sight. Would that it were. However, it was good of you to come so quickly.'

'I had been hoping to slip into Laguiole while I was in the area and visit Pierre Calmels' workshop,' said Monsieur Pamplemouse pointedly. 'I had in mind buying my wife a new kitchen knife for Christmas. Such a present from the oldest *coutellerie* in the town would have had a special cachet.'

'They do say the handle of traditional Laguiole knives is modelled on a young girl's thigh,' said Monsieur Leclercq dreamily.

Monsieur Pamplemousse resisted the temptation to point out that had been at the beginning of the nineteenth century, and history didn't record anything beyond the designer's name, which was Eustache Dubois. Clearly, the Director had his mind on other matters.

'It all began,' said Monsieur Leclercq, 'when I was returning from a recent visit to New York, where I had been attending a seminar on business efficiency. It was in the nature of a damage repair mission. Since what is still referred to as 9/11, there has been a noticeable slackening in the exchange of views between our two great nations, almost as though we were at war with each other. Windows belonging to French restaurants in Dallas have been smeared with noxious substances of a personal nature. Congress registered its displeasure by renaming French fries in its cafeterias "freedom fries" – a classic case of having their cake and eating it if ever there was one.

'Fortunately, it was only a temporary measure, but in the meantime sales of *Le Guide* have plummeted. I understand from a bookshop on Lexington Avenue they no longer have them on general display, but provide them under plain cover.'

'There will always be those, mostly on the East and West coasts, who like to regard France as their second home and will continue to visit us, come what may,' said Monsieur Pamplemousse. 'But sadly, for the time being they are in the minority and tend to keep that fact to themselves, especially, so I am told, when they are travelling across Middle America.'

Monsieur Leclercq nodded his agreement. 'Even then I might not have gone, but Véronique came up with a brainwave.

'I must confess that after a strenuous week immersed in statistics and high-pressure salesmanship I was looking forward to the flight home and a chance to relax. You come across such a diverse range of people when you fly, especially when you travel Première Classe: a captain of industry one week, a leading scientist another, president of an oil company the next, politicians of note, film stars…

'In my experience, the latter are often the worst; always showing their profile rather than looking out of the window, or making outrageous demands on the cabin staff just as the plane is about to land. Given half a chance some of them would want the whole cabin redecorated before they deign to come aboard.

'However, it was the first time I had ever found myself seated next to a nun...'

Monsieur Pamplemousse tried to picture it. 'Perhaps the good lady had been upgraded out of regard for her advancing years?' he suggested.

'I think not,' said the Director. 'If that were the case the person in charge of the check-in desk needed to have their eyes tested. She was a pretty little thing.'

'Aah!' If Monsieur Leclercq wanted to focus his subordinate's attention, he was going the right way about it. Tastes in these matters varied enormously, of course, and Monsieur Pamplemousse was the last person to set himself up as an arbiter in such matters, but one thing was certain; place the Director amongst a group of disparate members of the opposite sex and he would unerringly make a beeline for the one who had all the hallmarks of being a troublemaker.

It had happened more than once over the years. Those he had been wont to describe as a 'pretty little thing', taking pity on them because they were sitting in a corner all alone at a party, were invariably doing so because others around them recognised the signs and were all too aware of the fact that pretty little things were not necessarily to be trusted.

'She let fall the fact,' continued Monsieur Leclercq, 'that by a strange coincidence she had attended a similar course to mine. She intimated that she was acting as a financial adviser to the Vatican.'

'*The* Vatican?' repeated Monsieur Pamplemousse. 'In Rome?'

'There is only one Vatican as far as I am aware, Pamplemousse. I do not think it has branched out.'

Monsieur Pamplemousse pursed his lips and let out a sucking noise. It emerged rather louder than he had intended.

'You do not approve?' asked the Director.

'Dealing with the higher echelons of the Catholic Church is not without its dangers, monsieur.'

'You are thinking of what happened to that man who became known as God's Banker?' said the Director. 'His name escapes me...'

'Roberto Calvi,' said Monsieur Pamplemousse. 'He ended up hanging from a bridge over the River Thames in London. Half of his pockets stuffed full of foreign currency – mostly dollars and Swiss francs; the other half, as I recall, were packed with stones, presumably meant to weigh him down.

'The bridge was called Blackfriars. Rather apt considering Calvi was a member of P-2 – an association of Freemasons that has since been outlawed by the Italian authorities. Blackfriars also happens to be the registered name of a Masonic lodge; the washing of feet is part of their symbolic ritual. Presumably, whoever lowered him into position was hoping that would happen when the tide came in.'

'I did mention his demise in passing,' admitted Monsieur Leclercq. 'The young lady professed total ignorance of the affair. Clearly, she had led a sheltered life. I suspect she was embarrassed to think such things could take place in this day and age. In Naples, perhaps, where I am told the Mafia is showing signs of a resurgence, but not London.

'It only served to confirm what a nice person she was, although having said that, after what occurred later I doubt if she will be in line for promotion to higher echelons of the ecclesiastical profession...'

Monsieur Leclercq paused again as though reliving the moment. '...She had the white skin one associates with many of her calling...and her accent was intriguing...I assumed at first it was Italian, but when I essayed a few apposite phrases she clearly didn't understand a word I was saying. However, it was her eyes that caught my attention most of all. Partly because she had perfected the trick of crossing them from time to time, seemingly at will, but also because they matched the grey leather strap belonging to her watch; a Baume & Mercier – one that has the dial actually concealed beneath the strap on the *inside* of the wrist. You may have seen them advertised. I had been thinking of getting my wife one for Christmas, but I have since had second thoughts. In view of what transpired, she may put two and two together. In any case, she prefers gold to silver.'

'Perhaps the young lady finds it helpful when she is carrying out her devotions,' said Monsieur Pamplemousse, feeling some encouragement might be due as Monsieur Leclercq went quiet again. 'It probably enables her to keep a surreptitious eye on the time.

'I once sat next to a nun,' he mused. 'It was on a Greek aircraft flying from Athens to one of the many islands in the Mediterranean, and it was not a happy experience. She began counting her worry beads as soon as the "fasten your seat belt" sign came on and she didn't stop until the man at the top of the disembarkation steps tapped on the aircraft door to signal it was safe to emerge. I have tried to avoid nuns ever since.'

'Very wise,' said Monsieur Leclercq. 'In my experience, conversation with ladies of the cloth is mostly limited to basic pleasantries. You can hardly say "have you read any good books lately?" since one assumes the Good Book is a necessary part of their daily devotions.

'One thing you can safely count on when travelling Première Classe is that on the whole passengers share a common interest in the food, a subject that hardly seems appropriate to someone living in a nunnery. Although having said that, despite her slender form she did ample justice to everything that came her way.

'I thought at first she was rather standoffish, and I didn't doubt she felt the same way about me. Having exchanged the usual pleasantries when we boarded...I was occupying 1A as usual, and she was in 1B, I suppose we were each doing our own thing before take-off. She was looking out of the window and as soon as we were given clearance I used my mobile to telephone Chantal and say I was on my way. The Première Classe seats on the Airbus 330 get wider and further and further apart these days...'

'I have seen pictures of them in flight magazines,' said Monsieur Pamplemousse. 'When I have had enough room to turn the pages, that is. If you are seated in the back of the plane and have the misfortune to be sandwiched between two passengers who are what your American friends would call "horizontally challenged", it is not always easy.'

Monsieur Leclercq stared at him suspiciously for a moment or two. 'Is that so, Pamplemousse? I find that hard to picture.

'Shortly afterwards,' he continued, 'our glasses of Dom Perignon '90 were replenished, along with a serving of caviar as an appetiser; a foretaste of things to come. I remember being impressed by the fact that despite all the talk of trade embargoes, it was still Beluga. From its taste, undoubtedly the product of an older sturgeon which, as you know, produces the best-quality roe. Perhaps the helping was rather less generous than one has grown accustomed to over the years, but that is by the by…'

'I have noticed the complimentary bags of peanuts are getting smaller too,' said Monsieur Pamplemousse. 'It makes them difficult to open. The less space you have at your disposal the harder it is. If you are not very careful, the bag bursts and they go everywhere.'

Monsieur Leclercq removed a handkerchief and dabbed at his forehead.

'We all have our problems, Pamplemousse,' he said shortly. 'The point I am leading up to is that that was when it happened…' He paused yet again, as though searching for exactly the right words before continuing.

Monsieur Pamplemousse hazarded a guess. 'The plane hit an air pocket and you cut your mouth on the tin of caviar? Or did the plastic spoon go in your eye?'

It would account for the dark glasses.

Monsieur Leclercq stared at him. 'As always,' he said stiffly, 'the caviar was served on Limoges china, and that in turn was resting on a bed of ice. The spoons, I may add, were made of horn rather than plastic, as indeed they should be.'

'Don't tell me you were poisoned, monsieur. These things happen…one can never be sure what goes on in the backstreets of Russia – especially those adjacent to the Urals. Corruption is rife since the Mafia became involved…also the more one hears about pollution of the Caspian Sea… You may have been mistaken for a mid-European diplomat, or presidential material. Remember what happened to that Ukrainian president before he was elected.'

Monsieur Leclercq stared at him. 'The caviar was from Petrossian,' he said simply. 'Their name is synonymous with the very best, their choice of sturgeon second to none, approved of by connoisseurs the world over. I enquired of the cabin crew. They all swore they ate nothing else. In any case, it had nothing to do with food poisoning. Would it were that simple.'

Once again, it struck Monsieur Pamplemousse that the Director was unusually ill at ease; the mopping of his brow had become more frequent.

'I'm not quite sure how it came about,' continued Monsieur Leclercq after a short pause, 'but my travelling companion appeared to be having trouble arranging the contents of her tray, and whilst trying to render assistance, somehow or other our heads collided. Vodka and caviar went everywhere – mostly over her habit.

'Unfortunately, the galley was behind us and the cabin staff had drawn the curtains across the aisle so that they could enjoy their own meal in peace. As I recall, following the caviar, whole fresh black Perigord truffles encased in pastry featured on the menu. The smell was already starting to permeate the cabin but alas, it was not to be.

'Not wishing to create a fuss and spoil their meal, my young neighbour covered her confusion admirably.

'We joked about how the good Dom Perignon, he who is credited with inventing champagne in the first place, might have reacted to the debacle.'

Monsieur Pamplemousse was tempted to suggest the good Dom might have been extremely cross had it been his first and only trial bottle, but the Director was by now in full spate.

'At the same moment as I reached down to retrieve her napkin, which had become detached from her bosom and fallen to the floor, I couldn't help but notice the top buttons of her habit were undone, revealing what I assumed at the time to be virgin territory. Her *mandarines*, Aristide, were in full view, each *pointe de sein* erect and protruding as though, despite the ambient temperature in the cabin, she had just stepped out of a cold shower.'

'It is extraordinary the amount of information one can glean in a split second,' said Monsieur Pamplemousse.

The Director eyed his subordinate suspiciously. 'It is all part of our training, Pamplemousse,' he said stiffly. 'No doubt when you sit down in a restaurant and your gaze alights on the table, you automatically experience much the same reaction: the arrangement of the cutlery; the juxtaposition of the knives, the forks and the spoons; the angle at which the wineglasses are set; the positioning of the condiments.'

Monsieur Pamplemousse couldn't help thinking the analogy was stretching his imagination more than somewhat, but he tried to look suitably rebuffed.

'I averted my gaze, of course,' continued Monsieur Leclercq, 'and as I did so she reached for her carry-on bag; a Louis Vuitton Antigua Cabas Shopper. I know, because my wife, Chantal, wants one, and despite the price there is a long waiting list. At the same moment I caught a waft of perfume, which momentarily threw me off guard...'

'Don't tell me,' essayed Monsieur Pamplemousse. 'Your heads collided again.'

'Worse that that,' said Monsieur Leclercq, gripping the edge of his desk as he relived the memory.

'By sheer chance our lips met and she held her own against mine. I cannot tell you what a heady moment it was as her tongue set out on a voyage of discovery.

'Believe me, Aristide, such explorations take on another dimension at 10,000 metres. It felt as though I was suddenly soaring heavenwards at the speed of light.'

I bet it did, thought Monsieur Pamplemousse, wondering where the conversation was heading.

'She turned out to be a charming girl,' continued the Director. 'She told me her name was Maria. Apparently, she was called that because at the time she was conceived her mother was watching a film called *The Sound of Music.*'

'On a home video, I trust,' said Monsieur Pamplemousse, 'and not in a cinema.'

Monsieur Leclercq chose to ignore the interruption. 'I assumed from her manner she was a novice, and I wondered if perhaps she had only recently taken the vow, possibly as the result of an unrequited love affair in her native land, and was now in need of some fatherly advice.

'However, she forestalled me by asking if by any chance I belonged to "The Mile High Club", and if not, would I care to join?

'It appears to be an exclusive organisation; membership is restricted to people such as myself who are frequent travellers, coming and going like ships that pass in the night.'

'Coming and going' struck Monsieur Pamplemousse as a singularly felicitous way of putting it.

'And did you?' he asked. 'Join, I mean.'

'Yes, and no,' said the Director. 'Possibly it had to do with her calling – the Vatican has a reputation for bureaucracy, but just as I was working out what the equivalent might be in kilometres, she revealed that it was necessary to undergo some kind of initiation ceremony. Apparently, it involved the use of water, much like a christening, so she suggested we repair to the toilet.

'Afterwards, she explained, I would be issued with a card. She happened to have one in an inner pocket of her habit. It had already been signed by the President...'

'Monsieur Sarkozy?'

'No, Pamplemousse,' said the Director testily. 'A lady also bearing the name Maria. Maria Monk, president of the club. It would simply require my signature, plus my companion's counter approval once the ceremony was over. My understanding was that membership entitled one to certain benefits at a chain of Parisian health clubs run by a graduate of the Corporeal Relaxation and Physical Stress Relief Department of the University of Bangkok.

'By then her outer garment required urgent attention – mopping up operations with the vodka and caviar was indicated, and since the cabin staff were still otherwise engaged, she suggested there was no time like the present and we could perhaps kill two birds with one stone by repairing to the toilet.

'She suggested I count up to ten and then follow on behind.'

'And?' Monsieur Pamplemousse felt himself on the edge of his seat. Even Pommes Frites was pricking up his ears.

'As things turned out,' said Monsieur Leclercq, 'I wish I had made it *soixante*. Things might have taken a different course had I given the cabin staff time to intervene.

'Once I was inside the toilet, she locked the door in order that we might remain undisturbed. I, of course, averted my gaze while she set about removing her outer garment, which I must admit did seem to be somewhat brief in view of the inclement weather we have been experiencing of late.'

'Perhaps,' ventured Monsieur Pamplemousse, 'the Vatican are also in the throes of an economy drive.' But he was wasting his breath.

'By chance,' continued the Director, 'I happened to catch sight of her reflection in a nearby mirror. Our eyes met and, turning her back, she edged towards me...

'I didn't know that nun's habits have a zip fastener that runs the entire length from top to bottom, did you, Aristide?'

Monsieur Pamplemousse had to admit he had never had occasion to investigate the matter.

'Well, hers did,' said the Director. 'And I tell you something else. When, at her invitation, I gave the catch a tug, it was like pulling the ripcord on a parachute. The garment billowed open, and as it floated to the ground she turned to face me, revealing yet another facet of her calling.

'Before that moment I could hardly have claimed familiarity with a nun's more intimate garments. Had I been asked for my views on the subject, I would have hazarded a guess at something sensible in calico with a double gusset, but a quick glance proved me wrong.

'I was appalled, Aristide; absolutely appalled. I had no idea they led quite such Spartan lives. The poor girl was singularly ill equipped for the rigours of winter. Apart from a token piece of gauzelike material, *culottes* were conspicuous by their absence. In short, to all intents and purposes she was as naked as the day she was born! I hardly knew where to rest my eyes.

'The only thing I couldn't help noticing was that she had a canal boat tattooed on her right *amortisseur*.'

Monsieur Pamplemousse stared at the Director. It was a long time since he had heard the word. He wondered where Monsieur Leclercq had been all these years.

'Perhaps it was a stick-on,' he suggested. 'The tattoo, not the *nibard*.'

The Director stared at him. 'What will they think of next?' he exclaimed.

'By then the poor girl was distraught. I comforted her as best I could, but she kept emitting moaning noises as though in the throes of some ghastly visitation. I even lent her my handkerchief. That was a mistake, of course. When I eventually retrieved it, there was lipstick everywhere.

'I offered to lend her my jacket, but that only seemed to make matters worse.

'She gave me another kiss and said she had never met anyone quite like me before.

'This time, when our lips met it had quite the opposite effect to the first occasion. It felt as though we were plunging earthwards.

'Can you guess why, Pamplemousse?'

'You had slipped on some soap, monsieur?'

'Nothing that simple,' said the Director.

'By then we were both on the floor. She was lying on top me and as I tried to disentangle myself, it happened again.

'I became dimly aware of the Captain issuing an urgent warning over the loudspeaker system to the effect that the plane had entered an area of high turbulence. He was advising everyone to return to their seats.'

'Saved by the bell, monsieur.'

'No, Pamplemousse,' said Monsieur Leclercq. 'As things turned out, quite the opposite. In truth, I would have liked nothing better than to obey his instructions.

'Almost immediately, someone began knocking on the door, calling out to the girl, asking her if she was all right.

'I have to say, Pamplemousse, comparisons are odious, but for all their relative size and luxury, the toilets in Première Classe are as devoid of anywhere to hide as I imagine they must be in at the rear of the plane.'

'I would think even more so,' said Monsieur Pamplemousse, trying to picture the scene. 'I have often noticed that those who have the misfortune to be "girth stricken" have to back out the same way as they went in.'

'A moment later,' continued the Director, 'the door flew open and I saw the Chief Steward gazing down at us. I had no idea until then that they have a special key for emergencies. I could tell by the look on his face that he had jumped to entirely the wrong conclusion.

'As he helped me to my feet I protested my innocence. Taking a leaf out of your book, Pamplemousse, I sought refuge in that age-old ploy you once apprised me of. I explained that my daughter was backpacking around the world, and I intimated that if any suggestions to the contrary were made I would refer the whole matter to my lawyers. I then lent Maria my mobile and suggested she telephone her mama, telling her there was nothing to worry about and that she was on her way home.

'The poor girl seemed confused at first. Possibly it had something to do with her eye problem, or the inclement conditions, but she kept pressing the wrong button and operating the camera flash by mistake. It was most embarrassing.

'Eventually, having managed to calm her down, I stood

back and left her to dial a number at random, while I tried to think of what to do next.'

Monsieur Pamplemousse nodded approvingly. 'As Pasteur was fond of saying, monsieur, chance favours the prepared mind.'

'That may have been true in Pasteur's case,' said the Director grimly, 'but it certainly did *me* no favours.

'I have to say Maria played her part as to the manner born. As soon as contact was established she assumed a child-like voice, full of girlish squeals. She went through the whole gamut about how she had never had such a lovely time in her life, and how happy she was. "Now I will hand you over to Papa." she trilled at last, handing me the mobile.'

'And?'

'What is the worst thing you can say to a woman on the other end of a telephone, Aristide?'

'There is nothing whatsoever to worry about, *cherie*?' suggested Monsieur Pamplemousse.

'*Exactement!*' said the Director. 'You have hit the nail on the head, Aristide. In my experience there is no surer way of arousing a woman's suspicions than by ringing her up out of the blue and saying there is no need to worry. Although in the event I didn't even get that far.

'You cannot possibly imagine the stream of vituperation that greeted me when I put the receiver to my ear.'

'But surely, monsieur, you only had press the OFF button to cut the call. The person at the other end would never have guessed who you were. Even if they had, what did it matter? You were over 10,000 metres up in the air over the Atlantic Ocean.'

'It matters a great deal, Pamplemousse,' said the Director

soberly, 'when it happens to be your wife. That is something not even Pasteur, for all his knowledge and worldly wisdom, could have prepared his mind for. Like me, he might well have wished he was on the ocean bed, rather than 10,000 metres above it.'

'I fully understand, monsieur, that what you have just told me could not have been the best news in the world, but...'

'There are no "buts" about it, Pamplemousse,' said the Director grimly. 'It was the worst possible news. Furthermore, it was only the tip of the iceberg.'

'You mean, there is worse to come?'

'That is putting it mildly,' said Monsieur Leclercq. 'It was not what our American friends would call a "marriage enhancing" situation. Fortunately, by the time I recognised Chantal's voice I was thinking on my feet. It made me appreciate what it must be like for a boxer when he finds himself up against the ropes with no means of escape, and the eyes of the world are upon him. Think how much worse it was in the confines of an Airbus galley, Aristide. At the time, I thought I acquitted myself well.

'As soon as I was able to get a word in edgeways I assumed an American accent and turned what might have been a debacle into a failure-deferred success. Peppering my speech with the latest transatlantic phraseology I had picked up during the human potential seminar, I began by apologising for my daughter's bone-head behaviour in dialling the wrong number.

'Then I went on to say it was my sincere hope madame wasn't feeling emotionally disrupted, or that she pictured me as some kind of crazy kook trying to pull a fast one by entering her life under the radar. I also made the point that I did not want her to think she had inadvertently become a pawn in a game plan which resulted in her feeling left off the loop. If that were the case, I would be happy to recommend a suitable anger evaluation consultancy...'

'And she understood what you were saying?'

'She was hanging on my every word,' said the Director. 'By the time I finished it was like having a pigeon eating out of my hand. A pigeon, moreover, cooing in a tone of voice I had not heard for many a year.

'Flushed with success, I suggested that since my daughter would be going straight back to finishing school once we landed, leaving me all on my own in little old Gay Paree, maybe the two of us could touch base.

'It was merely gilding the lily with a pleasantry, as it were. I had no intention of following it up, but she took the wind out of my sails. Do you know what she said, Aristide?'

Monsieur Pamplemousse shook his head.

'She said she would like nothing better, but we would have to exercise great care because her husband was due back shortly and he was apt to be extremely jealous.'

'You must have regretted your offer, monsieur.'

'On reflection, yes. But at the time, I was metaphorically still taking my bow. Acting is hard enough as it is, without the added burden of analysing the exact meaning of what one is saying.

'I have often suspected that the first actor to take the stage as Hamlet must have been playing for time when he uttered the immortal words "To be, or not to be", followed by a long pause. He had probably forgotten what came next.

'However, it was not for nothing, Aristide, that I once

played the part of Robespierre. It was not easy at the age of thirteen, but according to the school magazine I acquitted myself with flying colours.'

Monsieur Pamplemousse realised he had stepped into the trap. Over the years, the Director's oft-repeated tale had become the stuff of legends. One tended to forget he was at heart a frustrated thespian. Even in his youth, the part of 'Robespierre the Incorruptible' must have seemed like typecasting.

'Did it not worry you that the girl knew your home number, monsieur?'

Monsieur Leclercq shook his head. 'Thinking about it afterwards, I assumed she must have committed it to memory when I rang Chantal soon after boarding the plane.

'Being able to cross and uncross her eyes at will, I suspect she kept one of them fastened on my mobile while I was dialling, at the same time using the other eye to feign looking out of the window.'

'A useful faculty,' said Monsieur Pamplemousse dryly, 'but why would she do that?' Privately he remained sceptical. As he understood it, most people could only remember a maximum of nine digits. Ten-digit numbers were beyond them.

'I imagine for the same reason headlines in other people's *journaux* are invariably more interesting than one's own,' said the Director. 'Quite likely, her subconscious memory took over when it was her turn to dial a number. Given a free choice, some people's minds go blank.'

Monsieur Pamplemousse did his best not to look doubtful.

'Monsieur has wiped any photographs from his mobile, of course...'

Monsieur Leclercq shook his head. 'No, Pamplemousse. Monsieur has not.'

'If you have it with you, I will happily do it for you. It will only take a moment.'

'I am afraid it is too late,' said the Director. 'Unfortunately, following my performance, I was still on a slight high, so when the Captain announced that we were through the turbulence and we were no longer required to return to our seats, I placed the instrument on a convenient shelf...'

'Don't tell me it fell into the *gogue*, monsieur?'

'If by *gogue* you mean what I think you mean, Pamplemousse, the answer is no, more's the pity. At least, with a press of the button, it would be at the bottom of the Atlantic Ocean by now and it might have saved a lot of trouble. In the event, what transpired was far worse.

'I caught her inserting the wretched thing inside what passed for her *culottes*. As I mentioned earlier, it was the flimsiest garment I have ever seen; the kind of frilly object designed not so much to conceal, but rather to draw attention to that part of a lady's anatomy known in polite circles as *le duvet pubien*. It is a wonder it didn't fall out the other side.

'Having slipped into her habit, she then asked me if I would mind rendering assistance.

'I have to tell you, Aristide, as she bent over and presented me with a close up view of her *derrière*, the temptation to retrieve my mobile there and then was hard to resist, but chivalry won the day.

'In my haste to oblige I had scarcely reached the halfway stage when my tie became enmeshed in the teeth of her zip fastener. Given that it happened to be a birthday present from Chantal, I must confess panic set in. You know what wives are like. If they have given you an item of clothing and for some reason you don't wear it, they immediately take umbrage.'

'Ties are the very worst,' agreed Monsieur Pamplemousse. 'Especially if they have given you two. Whichever one you wear they inevitably ask what was wrong with the other.'

'It was, to say the least, a compromising situation, and the more I tugged, the worse it became. I could hardly call on the cabin staff, it would have stretched their credulity to breaking point. Fortunately, Maria reached into an inner pocket and, having produced a pair of scissors, suggested I used them to cut the end off, but only on one condition.'

'Which was?'

'I take her shopping and buy her a new outfit to replace the one that had been damaged.'

The Director paused as he caught sight of the expression on Monsieur Pamplemousse's face.

'I know what you are thinking, Aristide, but it is easy to be wise after the event. I was desperate at the time.

'I made arrangements there and then to meet her as soon possible after we got back to Paris.'

'So, all was well in the end.'

'It might have been, Aristide, had it not been for the fact that for the first time ever Chantal chose to meet me at the airport.'

'I wonder what made her do that?' said Monsieur Pamplemousse innocently.

'I have been wondering the same thing,' said Monsieur Leclercq. 'Unfortunately, my jacket was open. There are no prizes for guessing the first thing she noticed.'

'On the whole,' said Monsieur Pamplemousse, 'ladies do have an eye for these things.'

'Chantal is certainly no exception,' said Monsieur Leclercq. 'It was not a happy homecoming.'

'As a matter of interest,' said Monsieur Pamplemousse. 'What did happen to the end?'

'Maria asked if she could keep it as a souvenir,' said Monsieur Leclercq.

'Ah!' said Monsieur Pampleousse. It was all he could think of for the moment.

CHAPTER THREE

'I wonder,' ventured Monsieur Pamplemousse, 'do you think offering to take Maria out shopping might prove misguided in the long run?'

'Wondering doesn't enter into the calculation, Aristide,' said Monsieur Leclercq with feeling. 'It has already happened.

'I suppose in my mind's eye I pictured our meeting up at one of those small specialist shops which abound in the backstreets near the Bon Marché. However, in the event, her sights were fixed on higher things.

'She told me that in view of the nature of her work she had been given special dispensation by the Vatican to wear the kind of garments that would allow her to mingle freely with those engaged in the world of international banking. With that in mind, she suggested we rendezvous at Christian Dior.'

'Not the first name that springs to mind when one is thinking of buying ecclesiastical garments,' agreed Monsieur Pamplemousse.

'It would be if you happened to be my wife,' said the Director glumly. 'There are times when I strongly suspect she has shares in Dior, along with various other establishments in the area. It is where she spends most of her time whenever she goes shopping.

'That being so, it was almost inevitable that while Maria was viewing the current season's offerings, I caught sight of Chantal attempting to back her car into an empty space on the far side of the Avenue Matignon.

'Fortunately, parking does not come naturally to her at the best of times. Even from where I was standing, the gap was obviously a good ten centimetres less than the length of her car, so time was on my side.'

'The female mind works in a totally different way to that of the male,' said Monsieur Pamplemousse sympathetically. 'As I understand it, research shows they have different-shaped brains. It gives them the advantage over men in many respects, but not in others, parking being one of them.'

'I am not in the least surprised to hear it,' said Monsieur Leclercq. 'Their minds must be like the Place de la Concorde during the hour of affluence, with traffic going in all directions. Give Chantal a totally empty car park and she goes to pieces, driving round and round in ever decreasing circles asking *me* where she should leave it. Then she gets cross if I point out that she has control of the steering wheel.

'On the other hand, make no mistake about it, Aristide, had we encountered each other in Christian Dior that morning there would have been no question as to who was in the driving seat.

'Fearing that once she had found a suitable space she might head in our direction, I apprised Maria of the situation and suggested we make good our escape as quickly as possible. As I am sure you know, the House of Dior is a rabbit warren of interconnecting departments – a Heaven-sent arrangement in the circumstances – so we had no problem in that respect.

'Half an hour later, following a somewhat circuitous route, I found myself in a maze of unfamiliar streets near the Odeon. To do Maria justice, as we were about to enter an establishment called Maison Felicity, purveyor of ultra-sexy garments for today's sensual woman, she promised to return my mobile as soon as she had completed her purchases.'

'When you say circuitous, monsieur…'

The Director had the grace to look somewhat shamefaced.

'I mean, not as an average crow with an intimate knowledge of Paris would choose to fly were it in a hurry,' he said. 'First of all we visited a jeweller's in the rue St-Honoré…Maria had her eyes on something she had seen in their window…then we called in at Annick Goutal – a *parfumerie* in the Place St-Sulpice.'

Monsieur Pamplemousse couldn't resist it. 'Did you encounter many other nuns on your travels?' he asked.

'No, Pamplemousse,' said the Director testily. 'We did not. I must admit I was glad to reach the relative safety of Madame Felicity's; a charming lady, most welcoming. She even offered me a glass of Roederer Crystal champagne while I was waiting.

'Unfortunately, she had hardly finished pouring it when the worst happened. Maria happened to glance out of the window and thought she saw my wife approaching.'

'Did Chantal see you, monsieur?'

'She didn't get the chance. Reacting with commendable promptitude, Maria bundled me into one of the changing rooms and advised me not to come out again until she had given the all clear.

'I tell you something, Aristide; you have no idea of the things women talk about when they think no one of the opposite sex can overhear them. Technical details regarding other people's anatomy, their lover's, and in some cases that of their husband's too. I was forced to listen while comparisons were made and the most intimate details exchanged, and having listened, I did not dare emerge for fear of what their reaction might be.'

'A salutary experience, monsieur. You might have been scarred for life.'

'While I was incarcerated,' continued Monsieur Leclercq, 'I started to run over various things in my mind. I hesitate to say it, but for one reason and another I began to wonder if perhaps Maria is as virtuous as she would have me believe. Could it be, I asked myself, that her own regard for chastity was on a par with the others I could hear talking?'

Monsieur Pamplemousse stared at the Director. He never ceased to be amazed. There, on the one hand, stood a man of the world – a high-flyer in every sense of the word, always immaculately groomed: suits from André Bardot, ties from Marcel Lassance, handcrafted shoes from JW Weston, purveyors of footwear to successive presidents of France.

In earlier times he would probably have spent his Sunday afternoons strolling in the Bois de Boulogne; the epitome of a well-dressed roué about town. While doing so, he might well have encountered one of Maria's forebears, an *entraineuse* plying for custom on horseback rather than from a seat in the first-class cabin of a jumbo jet.

But clothes don't necessarily make the man. On the other side of the coin, there were times when he ought not to be allowed out alone, and his journey back from America had been one of them.

Part of the trouble was that he led a rarefied existence, so work-obsessed the simple pleasures of life passed him by. He wondered how long it was since Monsieur Leclercq had last seen a film other than on an aeroplane, or when he had taken an *autobus* or travelled on the Metro. He didn't begin to know the meaning of the word streetwise.

'Whatever makes you say that, monsieur?' he ventured.

'Little things, Pamplemousse,' said Monsieur Leclercq. 'Not least being the fact that when I finally emerged from the changing room of my own accord, Maria was no longer to be seen. I thought things had gone very quiet. Madame Felicity was getting ready to close and had actually forgotten I was there.'

'It is a pity you were not in Le Bon Marché, monsieur. I have it on good authority their changing rooms are equipped with telephones for the benefit of any customers who are in need of assistance. You could have called for help long before then.'

'Unfortunately, Aristide, such cutting-edge technology has yet to reach the 5th *arrondissement*.'

'And your mobile?'

'Maria had the grace to leave me a note. Not only that, but she made me a present of a new telephone. She said the old one had become irretrievably damaged...'

'You must have been very relieved,' said Monsieur Pamplemousse.

'It was a kind thought,' agreed the Director. 'Only marred, I might say, by the not inconsiderable bill from Madame Felicity, which was attached to the book of instructions.'

'So you are back where you started, monsieur.'

Monsieur Leclercq hesitated. '*Oui*, Aristide, and then again, *non*.

'I have to admit that all has not been well in the Leclercq household since I arrived back from America. The fact that the end of my tie was missing was only one item in a long list of problems. Placating Chantal has been a costly exercise.

'However, that is now by the by. There are a number of much more important issues we need to discuss.'

Rising to his feet, he picked up a remote control, reopened the sliding door leading to the balcony, and led the way outside. Not wishing to be left out of things, Pommes Frites followed on behind.

The Director didn't utter another word until he had made certain the door was safely closed behind them. Even then, he looked uneasy and began making faces, as though attempting to come to terms with whatever it was he had on his mind. For several moments not a word passed his lips.

Pommes Frites put his tail between his legs and looked the other way.

'What I have to say, Pamplemousse,' he began at long last, 'has to be treated with the utmost confidence. It must not, under any circumstances, reach ears other than your own.

'Looking out from this balcony,' he continued, abruptly changing the subject, 'what do you see?'

Monsieur Pamplemousse paused for a moment or two while gathering his thoughts. Alive, as always, to the prevailing atmosphere, Pommes Frites relaxed. Assuming one of his more thoughtful expressions, and following the direction of his master's eyeline, he placed his front paws on the balcony rail and stared into space, clearly hoping he might be of some assistance.

'Different people see different things,' said Monsieur Pamplemousse. 'Personally, gazing out over the rooftops of Paris and seeing it all laid out before me like some giant oriental carpet, has always been one of the great pleasures of life. I count myself lucky that I am able to do so from the balcony of my apartment in Montmartre. From here I get what is in effect a mirror image.

'Immediately in front of us lies the Esplanade des Invalides, with its avenues of lime trees on either side, and to its right, the Hôtel des Invalides, home to Napoleon's tomb.

'Beyond the Esplanade there is the Seine, and beyond that again lies the Avenue des Champs Élysées, with the Place de la Concorde at one end and the Arc de Triomphe at the other.

'I see the Jardin des Tuileries and the Opera, where, unknown to most passers-by, five hives on the roof above the stage house over 100,000 bees. During the season their search for nectar takes in not only the chestnut trees in the Champs Élysées, but the linden trees behind the Palais Royal, along with acacias and sophoras lining the Péripherique. Some even stray as far afield as the Bois de Boulogne.

'You can buy the result of their labours in the Opera House shop and in Fauchon...'

'Yes, yes, Pamplemousse,' said Monsieur Leclercq impatiently, 'that is all very interesting, but what else do you see?'

'What else?' repeated Monsieur Pamplemousse. 'Well, beyond the Opera and the Madeleine, across an ocean of blue rooftops and pink chimney pots, I see Montmartre, where Pommes Frites and I often walk together of a morning, and where long, long ago Saint Denis is said to have picked up his head after he was decapitated by the soldiery, and carried on heading north with it under his arm.'

'How very inconvenient for him,' said the Director. 'It is a miracle he could see where he was going.'

'There is a statue commemorating the fact,' said Monsieur Pamplemousse stoutly. 'It is by the fountain where he supposedly washed away the blood before moving on.

'Above all, I see a city where the old happily rubs shoulders with the new. Here and there on the surface, Monsieur Hector Guimard's original *fin de siècle* entrances to the Metro still stand – there is one at Abbesses, again near where I live, while below ground, on the Météor line, high-speed driverless trains whisk passengers to and fro between the Gare St Lazare and the Bibliotech Nationale.

'It is much like a very grand child's play area contained within the bowl of the surrounding hills.

'As for Pommes Frites, it is hard to know what he sees, or indeed what he is thinking. I suspect he is not greatly concerned with landscapes. I have often noticed when we are out driving that he is more interested in things immediately in front of his eyes; trees and lampposts, the occasional rabbit. At this very moment, for example, he is probably taking note of the men playing boules on the Esplanade, or the lady who is going past with a Dandie Dinmont tucked under one arm...'

Realising the Director's eyes had a somewhat glazed look about them, Monsieur Pamplemousse's voice trailed away.

'Interesting, Pamplemousse,' said Monsieur Leclercq, 'very interesting; particularly if you happen to be writing a guide book. You are, of course, absolutely correct when you say Paris means different things to different people. Allow me to tell you what it means to me.

'In my mind's eye I see well over a thousand hotels and restaurants listed in *Le Guide*. On a clear day, with the aid of my telescope, I am able to locate over one hundred that have been awarded one or more Stock Pots.

'Sixteen of them have two Stock Pots. They include the oldest restaurant in Paris, La Tour d'Argent, which has been in existence since 1582; not so many years after the death of Christopher Columbus. It was there that an eating implement called the fork was first introduced to Parisian diners, and it is on record that the Duke of Richelieu once hosted a party during which a whole ox was cooked in thirty different ways.

'I can pick out Taillevent in the rue Lamenais; under Monsieur Vrinat, without doubt the best run restaurant in the world. Nearby, I see Pierre Gagnaire, one of the more innovative chefs of our time, and with the further aid of the brass plate set in the balustrade, I can locate the remaining eight who have been awarded the supreme accolade of Three Stock Pots in *Le Guide*.'

Monsieur Leclercq broke off.

'And that is only Paris, Pamplemousse. There is the rest of France to consider. We should be proud of the small part we have played in their owner's success, but it is a heavy responsibility nevertheless.

'There are times when I lie awake wondering if we are doing any restaurateur a favour by awarding him or her three Stock Pots, especially when you think of all it entails.'

'If I may say so,' said Monsieur Pamplemousse, 'it is their chosen vocation.'

'That is indeed true,' said the Director, 'but by the same token we have chosen to act as their judge and jury. Assessing all the evidence every year and reaching a verdict on the many hotels and restaurants appearing in *Le Guide* is no easy task.'

'The pursuit of excellence is never easy,' mused Monsieur Pamplemousse. 'If a thing is worth doing at all, it is worth doing well.'

'Absolutely,' said Monsieur Leclercq. 'But afterwards they have to live with the certain knowledge that others, including many they have trained, are coming up fast behind them. They cannot afford to rest on their laurels as the ancient Greeks so wisely put it.

'Other than being a head of state, there are few areas where the pressures are greater than in the world of haute cuisine; a film director perhaps, a prima ballerina, an opera singer…

'It is to the credit of French chefs that they have always treated food with respect. Carême set down the guiding principles in his vast twelve-volume work, elevating gastronomy to an art form destined to take its place alongside painting and music. The highest honour you can bestow on a person is to name something after them; in the case of cuisine, a dish such as Pêche Melba.

'But, to stay in front of the pack you have to innovate. Some engage a full-time PRO, others open up less expensive clones, some try to duplicate their success abroad, in countries like Japan and America. Some put their names to packaged foods; others dabble in all four at the same time.'

Monsieur Pamplemousse glanced round at the Director. He wondered where the conversation was leading. Clearly, he had not been ordered back simply to talk about the problems of running a restaurant. It had to be something much nearer home; internal problems with *Le Guide* perhaps? Surely… surely Monsieur Leclercq wasn't allowing it to get to him to such an extent he was heading for a breakdown.

He decided to take the bull by the horns.

'I have always prided myself on running a happy ship,' said Monsieur Leclercq, in answer to his question. 'Tight, but happy, and as with all great leaders, I have made the well-being of those under me my number one priority.'

Monsieur Pamplemousse wondered. He didn't doubt the Director's sincerity, but his remarks put him in mind of the late President Mitterand.

When asked what quality a great statesman needed most, his answer had been 'indifference'. In his view, nothing really mattered except his own political career. He maintained it had a knock-on effect. Upon his success depended the well-being of others.

But then he was a supreme pragmatist, which wasn't the same as being selfish.

'Currently,' continued Monsieur Leclercq, assuming the ensuing silence meant tacit agreement on the part of Monsieur Pamplemousse, 'currently, I am being assailed on all sides; both from within and from without.

'Shortly before you arrived, my wife telephoned to say she had taken delivery of a bouquet of flowers courtesy of the airline, along with a letter apologising for all the trouble I had met with on the flight back from New York.'

'But surely, monsieur, that was only good public relations.'

'They were addressed to my daughter,' said Monsieur Leclercq.

'We have weathered worse storms,' he continued philosophically. 'Force 8 gales are not unknown in the Leclercq household. It usually ends in my having to underwrite a spending spree on her wardrobe.'

'Most marriages have their bad moments; their little misunderstandings,' said Monsieur Pamplemousse. '*C'est la vie*. It is all part of life's rich tapestry, as the saying goes.'

'I agree,' said Monsieur Leclercq. 'And on a personal level I can cope with such problems, but when it is something that threatens to affect the reputation of *Le Guide*, it is an entirely different matter.

'I can no longer grass over the fact that some*one* or some *body* has launched a three-pronged attack on us. As far as the internal workings of *Le Guide* is concerned, there is a whispering campaign; rumours, as you rightly say, are rife. They are for the most part totally untrue, but they are having a devastating effect on staff morale.

'Worse still, and much more worrying, is the fact that someone has been infiltrating our files. Nothing major, as happened on the previous occasion – simple things, more a matter of additions and subtraction, but for that reason alone they are potentially more dangerous.

'For example, the entry for Tour d'Argent no longer makes mention of their *canard*. When my wife and I last dined there our duck was numbered 1,027,078 – and they only began numbering them in 1890! As for the wine list, it simply recommends a demi-carafe of the house red.

'That, in a restaurant whose cellars boast over 400,000 bottles, enumerated in a wine list that is larger than most family bibles.'

'That *is* serious, monsieur.'

'Serious, yes, but not fatal. Worse, much worse, are the additions. Egg and chips figures largely in lists of specialities. Imagine the reaction at the Tour d'Argent had they seen it starring as their main signature dish.'

'It doesn't bear thinking about,' said Monsieur Pamplemousse.

'Another thing, Pamplemousse. Have you encountered the family *Cimicidae* in your travels?'

'I don't think we have met,' said Monsieur Pamplemousse. He was having difficulty in keeping up with the Director's constant changes of direction. He watched as the other removed a folded sheet of paper from his wallet, and held it up for him to see.

Although only in silhouette form, the character depicted was indeed a fearsome sight; reminiscent of the notorious Tarasque of Tarascon, a hideous monster with six paws, a serpent's tail, and an insatiable taste for human flesh.

'If that is the patron, he looks like a wanted poster for a rapist of the very worst kind,' he said. 'The suggestion of tusks doesn't help matters. It is like Frankenstein without the terminals. It's a wonder he has any customers at all.

'It is not a *he*,' said the Director impatiently.

'Well,' said Monsieur Pamplemousse, 'If it is Madame Cimicidae, then I wouldn't like to meet her on a dark night. It could be Lucretia Borgia when she had one of her headaches; very off-putting.'

The Director clicked his teeth impatiently.

'Sex doesn't enter it, Pamplemousse. Bedbugs have other ways of satisfying their appetites. It has entered *Le Guide* as our latest symbol.'

'A bedbug!' Monsieur Pamplemousse peered at the picture with renewed interest.

'I think I can honestly say that in all the years I have worked for *Le Guide*, I have never encountered one.'

'At yesterday's count,' said Monsieur Leclercq grimly, 'over

1000 hotels listed in *Le Guide* are now credited with being home to them. The symbol you are looking at has been sprinkled at random throughout the text like confetti on a windy day.

'Had it been allowed to go through unchecked we would have been made a laughing stock. Untold harm could have been done to the tourist trade. Writs would have been flying right, left and centre. Fortunately we caught it in the nick of time, but we need to remain focused.

'We must take action, Pamplemousse. Failure is not an option. With the new edition already in the pipeline, time is not on our side. It is essential we find out as soon as possible who is behind it all.'

'You don't suspect any of the other guides?' asked Monsieur Pamplemousse.

'Dog eating dog?' The Director dismissed the idea. 'I think not. Our nearest rival is Michelin, and they would never stoop to such a thing. Besides, they have had their own share of troubles recently.

'There was the unhappy occasion when they awarded rosettes to a restaurant in Belgium that hadn't even opened. The whole edition had to be pulped.'

'A singularly unfortunate oversight on someone's part,' said Monsieur Pamplemousse dryly.

'These things happen even in the best-regulated houses,' said Monsieur Leclercq.

'However, it is something we couldn't possibly afford. We do not enjoy the same financial backing as Michelin. They enjoy the luxury of having their tyre sales to fall back on; as large and as comfortable as Monsieur Bibendum himself.

'We rely solely on the proceeds from the sale of *Le Guide* to those people who are looking for somewhere suitable to stay and who are interested in food.

'Then there was all the fuss when one of their inspectors wanted to write a book about what he chose to call "goings-on behind the scenes"…'

'An ex-inspector,' corrected Monsieur Pamplemousse. 'Pascal Rémy.'

'*Exactement.* We shall never know the truth. They also value anonymity, although perhaps not quite as strictly as we do.

'Unlike Michelin, we do not announce where we are from at the end of a meal. It has been that way ever since that ill-fated occasion soon after I joined *Le Guide* when I revealed the purpose of my visit to the owner of a restaurant in Belfort who was passing off a run-of-the-mill chicken as Poularde de Bresse. If you recall, he tried to murder me. After that our founder made total anonymity the rule.'

'And Gault Millau?'

'There was a time when they made us all look to our laurels. Their off-beat reports and their inspired journalistic use of the term "nouvelle cuisine" set the pace for a while. But since the two partners retired, it has had more owners than Elizabeth Taylor has had husbands.

'For a time Pudlowski was our main rival in Paris, but now he has made the quantum leap to covering the whole of France he has his hands full.

'No, Pamplemousse, other forces are at play, and we must on no account give way to them.

'*Le Guide*'s responsibility is twofold. Firstly, to the reader. Secondly, and of equal importance, we owe it to the establishments we choose to recommend. We must offer them our support and encouragement. In order to do that, we not only need to preserve our independence, but in order to criticise others, we must be above criticism ourselves.'

A sudden gust of wind sent odd scraps of paper flying in the street below them, effectively bringing all conversation to an end.

The Director gave a shiver, pressed the remote control to open the sliding doors, then turned abruptly on his heels and led the way back into his office.

Monsieur Pamplemousse signalled Pommes Frites to follow.

Pausing for a moment while he operated the sliding door, Monsieur Leclercq gazed reverently at the founder's portrait.

'Above all, Aristide,' he said, 'we must not let *him* down. Probity is the word I am seeking. Probity was Monsieur Hippolyte Duval's middle name, and no matter what, we must ensure *Le Guide* continues to reflect the high standards he laid down all those years ago.

'In the words of the President of the United States of America, Pamplemousse,' he said grandly, '"Failure to do so will not happen on my watch".'

Monsieur Pamplemousse began to wish he hadn't mentioned Napoleon earlier. As it was, the Director suffered from an image issue, but the close proximity of the Emperor's tomb often brought out the worst in him.

'Perhaps,' he said thoughtfully, 'we should take heart from the fact that even Monsieur Duval's life wasn't entirely blameless.'

He glanced up at the portrait, remembering the occasion when Monsieur Leclercq had instructed him to deliver a Renault Twingo to an address in Roanne, where the founder's illegitimate daughter lived. You never could tell.

As he had said at the time, 'Still waters run deep'.

The point went home.

'The reason our founder never married,' said the Director simply, 'was because he was too immersed in his work. He was approaching sixty years of age when, for what was probably the first and only time in his life, he strayed from the path of righteous behaviour. And that only came about because he was taken ill while snowbound at a small hotel in the Auvergne.

'It was hardly his fault the landlady's daughter climbed into bed with him before he was fully recovered. After a lifetime of abstinence, he must have had a lot bottled up.

'Weakened as he was by the after-effects of influenza, it is all too easy to see how he must have found her blandishments hard to resist. By all accounts she was a comely girl.'

'The winters are long and hard in the Auvergne,' said Monsieur Pamplemousse.

'The inhabitants have to do something to pass the time.'

'You should know, Aristide,' said the Director pointedly. 'But never forget, in the early days, our founder went everywhere on his Michaux *bicyclette,* and that was before the invention of the pneumatic tyre and sprung saddles. It might have played havoc with his manhood. At least, in later life, having traded his *bicyclette* in for an eight-cylinder Delage, he got it out of his system and in so doing proved the opposite to be the case.

'As the English poet Donne famously said: "To err is human, to forgive is divine".'

'I am always telling my wife that,' said Monsieur Pamplemousse sadly. 'I am not sure she is in total agreement with his philosophy. She calls it "poet's licence".'

'How many of us,' said Monsieur Leclercq pointedly, 'can say, hand on heart, we have only strayed but once in our lives?'

'You mentioned a third prong,' continued Monsieur Pamplemousse, hastily changing the subject.

'Ah,' said the Director. 'It is one of the main reasons why I sent for you, Aristide.' He paused to mop his brow.

Clearly ill at ease, and, despite his words, looking far from pleased at being reminded of the task in hand, he rummaged in a desk drawer and produced a bundle of photographs. Riffling through them, he singled out one near the bottom of the pile.

'This arrived on my desk yesterday morning. Fortunately, it came by special courier and was addressed to me personally, otherwise...'

Monsieur Pamplemousse braced himself, wondering what he was about to see.

'It grieves me more than I can possibly tell you, Aristide,' said Monsieur Leclercq, 'but you do realise, of course, that in our founder's day this kind of behaviour would have resulted in your instant dismissal.'

Monsieur Pamplemousse stared at the photograph. It showed the inside of a restaurant and bore many of the telltale signs of having been taken on a mobile phone.

A small section of the original must have been blown up out of all proportion. Pixels were in short supply.

'It is a good one of Pommes Frites,' he admitted, holding it down for him to see. 'He looks very pleased with life.'

'As well he might be,' said the Director grimly. '*Poularde de Bresse en Vessie*, if I am not mistaken. Helped on its way by a bottle of Montrachet. I trust it was a good year.'

'I remember the occasion,' said Monsieur Pamplemousse defensively. 'We were in Lyon and I ordered the *poularde* because it is one of the chef's specialities. I was handing Pommes Frites his share while I thought no one else was looking. Clearly, I was mistaken, although why anyone would wish to take a picture of us, I don't know. May I keep it?'

Monsieur Leclercq heaved a deep sigh.

'I fear not, Pamplemousse,' he said severely. 'We may yet need it for what our lawyers will undoubtedly refer to as Exhibit "A" when a case is brought to court.

'As for why anyone should wish to photograph the scene in the first place, the answer is simple. It was sent to one of France's most illustrious *journaux*, along with an article by an unnamed freelance journalist. Fortunately, the editor happens to be an old friend of mine and he has promised to hold back on the story for the time being.

'The writer of the article stated categorically that we are in an even worse state than Michelin. He says we are now so short of inspectors we have had to resort to using dogs to do the field work for us!'

'But...' Monsieur Pamplemousse stared at the Director, 'that is ridiculous...'

'Ridiculous it may be,' said Monsieur Leclercq. 'However, you know as well as I do, Aristide, that once the media get hold of a story like that there will be no holding them. They will have a field day. Ultimately, it could spell ruin for *Le Guide*.'

'I would back Pommes Frites' opinion against anyone else you care to mention,' said Monsieur Pamplemousse loyally. 'His powers of observation are second to none. Many times over the years I have had to amend my reports following something he has noticed. It is not so much a question of taste – the food generally goes down at such a rate it barely touches the side of his throat. It is more a matter of scent. The preliminary sniff says it all. If there is anything the slightest bit untoward, you can forget it. I have often thought of writing an article on the subject of animals and food for the staff magazine.

'In fact,' he held the picture up to the light, 'this is the kind of shot Calvet is always on the look-out for the front cover of *l'Escargot*. He has a theory that once you have seen one snail you have seen the lot.

'That is not to criticise *Le Guide*'s logo of two *escargots* rampant,' he added hastily. 'But when they have their heads inside their shell it is hard to tell what they are thinking or, indeed, whether they are coming or going, and they probably feel the same way. I daresay Trigaux would be able to liven it up a bit in his lab. He loves getting his teeth into that kind of problem.'

'And what did Pommes Frites think of the wine?' asked Monsieur Leclercq pointedly. 'I haven't had your P38 report downloaded, Madame Grante is away at the moment, but it looks to me very much like an '86 from Sauzet. That is also one of his favourites, I presume?'

'We happened to be in a three Stock Pot establishment, monsieur; one that prides itself on its wine list. To have ordered a glass of the house white would have drawn attention to our table. Suspicions would have been aroused.'

'There is such a thing as a happy medium,' said the Director grumpily.

It struck Monsieur Pamplemousse that the rumours might be true and Monsieur Leclercq really was engaged in a financial blitzkrieg. The lack of a water bowl for Pommes Frites could be part of a cost-cutting exercise. However, there were limits.

Besides, it didn't gel with his engaging the services of a doubtlessly highly paid security guard at the gates.

He tried one last ploy. 'As you have so often pointed out in the past, monsieur, "good wine is never expensive, only bad wine".

'In any case,' he continued, 'Pommes Frites simply had his usual sniff of my glass under the table. That hardly counts as sharing. Apart from birthdays and Christmas, he is, to all intents and purposes, teetotal.'

'Others are not cognisant of that fact, Pamplemousse,' said the Director. 'For all they know he could have been on his second or third bottle.'

'Apart from a soupçon in his water bowl at Christmas, wine is not his particular forte, monsieur,' continued Monsieur Pamplemousse defensively. 'He is hardly in line to become an honorary member of Alcoholics Anonymous.

'Occasionally, if it is a vintage red that has thrown some sediment, he stretches a point and has a morsel on some bread for his memory bank, but that is as far as it goes. He prefers to keep his sensory perceptions unsullied by alcohol, honed and ready for action at all times.'

'All that may be true,' said the Director. 'However, I fear certain parallels can be drawn between the picture you are holding in your hand and Michelin's recent problem with the ex-member of staff we were talking about earlier.'

Monsieur Pamplemousse wondered if the same person could be responsible for the latest picture, but he kept his thoughts to himself.

'Clearly, monsieur,' he said, handing it back, 'there are problems that need to be addressed.'

Monsieur Leclercq's face cleared. 'I'm glad you are of like mind, Aristide. With that end in view I have engaged outside help.'

'So I am given to understand,' said Monsieur Pamplemousse warily.

'Speaking personally, I was fully prepared to put your case on the back boiler for the time being, but my adviser makes the very valid point that should the picture ever be published, your own anonymity, so precious when working for *Le Guide*, will be blown.

'In short, I fear Pommes Frites will have to go.'

Having finally made his point, Monsieur Leclercq busied himself with some papers on his desk.

For the second time that day, the principal subject of his words gave vent to his feelings. Seeing the picture of the chicken portions after the prolonged absence of any kind of food whatsoever since breakfast, was bad enough. Now, having caught sight of the look on his master's face, he simply couldn't help himself. His long drawn-out howl captured the prevailing mood in a way that mere words could never have achieved.

As for Monsieur Pamplemousse; he was temporarily struck dumb.

Monsieur Leclercq was quick to take advantage of the silence. 'It only serves to confirm the wisdom of the old adage, Aristide,' he said gently. 'There is no point whatsoever in buying a dog and then barking yourself.

'There is nothing more to add. Pommes Frites has said it all.'

Monsieur Pamplemousse took a deep breath as he rose to leave. 'In that case, monsieur,' he said, enunciating his words slowly and distinctly, thus leaving no room for doubt, 'you will have no further need of my services either. As I see things, it spells the end of the road for both of us. If monsieur would be kind enough to say when he wishes us to leave...'

Reaching for a notepad and pen, Monsieur Leclercq scribbled a few hasty words before glancing at his watch.

'I think now is as good a time as any, Pamplemousse,' he said, handing the scrap of paper across the table. 'Before you leave the building I suggest you clear your IN tray.'

Monsieur Pamplemousse pocketed the paper. 'That will not be necessary, monsieur,' he said stiffly. 'I went through it when we arrived. There is nothing outstanding.'

'That being the case,' said Monsieur Leclercq, 'I can but wish both of you *bonne journée*.'

CHAPTER FOUR

'Is anything the matter, Aristide?' asked Doucette. 'You've hardly touched your dinner. After all that rich food you've been eating over the past few weeks, I thought you might be glad of something more down to earth.'

Monsieur Pamplemousse raised his eyes heavenwards. It was one of the hazards of his occupation. In much the same way as an author renders himself an object of deep suspicion in the eyes of the tax authorities if he enters 'visits to the Folies-Bergère x 4' on his tax return while researching a book on folk dancing, so the commonly perceived view of anyone working as an inspector for *Le Guide* was that life must be one long gastronomic holiday.

Even one's nearest and dearest took it for granted you were living it up all the time, completely ignoring the simple fact that the ten thousand or so entries in *Le Guide* represented the cream of French cuisine. Reporting on the many others who, for one reason or another didn't make the grade, was the downside of the job.

Many small hotels, once the backbone of the business, had

fallen on hard times. The bedrooms, with their worn-out carpets and mattresses sporting a permanent dip in the middle, remained ice-cold in winter and sweltering hot during the summer months because their one-time mainstay, the *voyageurs commerces*, were themselves fighting a losing battle with customers who were now placing their orders via the Internet.

On the gastronomic side, it took no account of those restaurants whose over-elaborate menus meant only one thing; prefabricated frozen meals. Often, if the truth be known, well beyond their 'consume by' date.

To cap it all, at the end of every day, five hundred boxes in *Le Guide*'s questionnaire covering every item from Ashtrays in the bedroom to Zabaglione in the restaurant, had to be marked with a tick or a cross, comments being added where necessary.

'I'm sorry, Couscous,' he said. 'My mind was on other things.'

'Well,' remarked Doucette, 'whatever it was, Pommes Frites seems to have caught the bug as well. He's hardly touched his plate. Don't tell me he has his mind on other things as well. Just look at his face. Knowing he doesn't like fish, I got him something different.'

Monsieur Pamplemousse pulled himself together. Doucette was right. It must be extremely galling to go to so much trouble over a meal, only to have it treated with a lack of respect.

For the time being, he relegated his problems to what Monsieur Leclercq would have called the 'back burner'.

Doucette had chosen well. What he fondly called the 'prawn dish' fitted his mood after a long day behind the wheel; the bottle of white Corbières Vieilles Vignes from Roland Legard, just what the proverbial doctor might have ordered.

'Couscous,' he said, 'you are *une perle*; and adventurous with it, branching out into unknown territory all by yourself like this. The Languedoc is a vast area.'

Doucette went a becoming shade of pink. 'I am not married to a food inspector for nothing.'

Monsieur Pamplemousse returned to the matter in hand.

Although he had nicknamed it the 'prawn dish', he might just as well have called it the 'egg dish', or the 'one with the sliced tomatoes'; for all three ingredients were combined in separate layers. Enveloped in a cheese sauce, capped by a layer of breadcrumbs, and cooked in the oven until the top was golden brown, it was a dish for all seasons.

Spearing a particularly large prawn, he held it up to the light. '*Parfait!*' he exclaimed.

Their good friends, the Pickerings, whose recipe it was, maintained the dish was at its best in the early part of the year, when it could be accompanied by peas fresh from the garden and roast potatoes. But then, *les Anglais* were wedded to what they called their 'two veg'.

Being French, Monsieur and Madame Pamplemousse were content to accompany their version with a fresh green salad.

There were other minor differences of course; the prawns in particular were a good example. According to Mr Pickering, theirs were deep frozen and rarely, if ever, recovered their distinctive taste after being shelled by machine somewhere or other on the far side of the world, whereas the Pamplemousse's were sea-fresh from the local *poissonnier*.

But wasn't that so with most recipes? A flourishing industry had been built up satisfying the insatiable need of people who invested heavily in cookery books hoping that something magical would happen, only to blame anyone but themselves when it didn't. In the end it wasn't only a matter of fresh ingredients; the hands that melded them together were important too.

'I am very lucky', he said, 'that you have the touch, Doucette. It is something you were born with, unlike some.'

The 'unlike some', was a reference to her sister Agathe, who had certainly missed out on that score with her *tripes à la mode de Caen*. It was a case of being wise after the event, but in retrospect he often wished he hadn't been quite so lavish with his praise the first time they met when he had been on his best behaviour. From that moment on he had always been given it as 'a treat'

Realising he still hadn't answered his wife's question, he helped himself to a second portion while trying to condense the story into as few words as possible.

Doucette listened in silence until he reached the point where Monsieur Leclercq delivered his bombshell regarding Pommes Frites.

She gazed across the table at her husband.

'But can he do that? Surely there are laws…'

'Pommes Frites is not a member of staff,' said Monsieur Pamplemousse simply. 'He has no rights.'

'But that is terrible, Aristide. You cannot let it happen.'

'You see my dilemma, Couscous,' said Monsieur Pamplemousse. 'And to give the Director his due, I can see his side of the argument. That being the case, I have no alternative but to resign.

'Monsieur Leclercq is paranoid about his work. To him it is

the beginning and end of everything. The word "failure" has no place in his vocabulary. Were *Le Guide* to fail, the disgrace would kill him.'

'But surely,' said Doucette, 'things cannot be as bad as all that. Most businesses have their ups and downs. People have short memories. Given time, it will all blow over...'

'You don't know the half of it, Couscous,' said Monsieur Pamplemousse sombrely. 'For whatever reason, someone has it in for *Le Guide*. Feelings are running high within the company. So much so, cars are being daubed with graffiti. Such a thing would have been unheard of a few weeks ago.'

'It seems to me there are a great many sad people in this world who are out to destroy things merely for the sake of it,' said Doucette. '*Les tagueurs* cannot see anything beautiful without wishing to cover it with spray paint, just as there are others who can't bear to see something that is successful.'

'It is a worldwide problem,' said Monsieur Pamplemousse. 'Not made any easier because generally speaking the perpetrators are often hard to catch.

'In Grande Bretagne they have a theory that many of those who indulge in graffiti take pride in their work and want others to admire it, so whenever possible they erase it as quickly as possible, hoping that in the end they will give up.

'In France, we agree with the theory, but feel perhaps the perpetrators should be as it were, privatised, and given a place where they can display their talents to the public in a more civilised fashion; hence the recent exhibition in Paris with a top prize of €1,500.

'In America, science has been brought to bear on the problem. They have invented a device called the Tagger Trap. Strategically placed, it is activated by the fumes from spray cans which triggers off an alarm in the nearest police station.

'But these are relatively minor things. When it comes to big business, especially with an organisation like *Le Guide*, where accuracy is paramount, the problem is entirely different. Monsieur Leclercq is right. It takes years to build up a reputation, but mud sticks and it can be destroyed overnight.'

He speared another prawn.

'In many ways *Le Guide* is not unlike the recipe for this dish; it is the sum of its many parts. Take away one and the rot sets in.

'Currently, *Le Guide* is suffering from the presence of a suspect crustacea. Such a thing is insidious, for it only takes a single bad one to affect the whole.

'The culprit in this case is not hard to find. It comes in the shape of a so-called business efficiency expert; a person who, it seems, is able to come and go in their own time and is certainly in a position whereby they can put into effect all manner of little changes, many of which threaten to undermine the very foundations of what, until now, has been a happy and successful company.

'These things take root and in no time at all begin to multiply, growing like a cancer unless they are caught and dealt with at an early stage.

'It is what Monsieur Leclercq, fresh from his seminar in the United States, calls the "trickle down" effect.

'Madame Grante's refusal to come into the office is a prime example: according to Glandier, expense sheets are piling up, and that in turn means approval of claims is being delayed, which is no small matter.'

'But, surely...' Doucette could hardly contain her impatience, 'if you know the problem, the solution is easy.'

'I suspect it is more complicated than that,' said Monsieur Pamplemousse. 'I am only giving you the edited version.'

'You have met this so-called expert?' asked Doucette.

'Not yet,' said Monsieur Pamplemousse. 'And now, perhaps I never shall.'

He glanced down at the selection of cutlery left on the table. 'It is something I intend to get to the bottom of before too long, but in the meantime, what other delights have you in store for me tonight?'

'*Fruit de saison*,' said Doucette. 'Or *yaourt*.

'They are both very good for you,' she added, seeing the look on his face.

'Especially after all you have been eating. If only you had let me know you were coming I might have done better...'

'There has been a lot of catching up to do, Couscous,' said Monsieur Pamplemousse contritely. 'Talking of which, have there been any messages for me while we have been away?'

Doucette began clearing the table. 'Someone was enquiring after you the other day. They asked the concierge if you were still living here, but whoever it was, they didn't leave a name. He rang to tell me and I went out onto the balcony, pretending I was watering the plants, but I couldn't see anyone.

'Also, Véronique phoned. She would like to see you as soon as possible. She said she will be at home this evening...'

'When was that?' Monsieur Pamplemousse looked up in surprise.

'It must have been shortly after you left the office,' said Doucette. 'It sounded urgent, but I didn't say anything before because I know you. It would have spoilt your dinner. You would either have bolted it down as though there were no tomorrow or else gone without it altogether.'

Monsieur Pamplemousse drained his glass. 'As far as my problem with Pommes Frites is concerned, I am afraid the chief had a point,' he said. 'There is only one way to stop it. Find the person who sent the photograph, and take it from there.'

'Who could it possibly be?' said Doucette.

Monsieur Pamplemousse shrugged. 'Perhaps Véronique has some ideas.' Rising from the table, he disconnected his phone, which had been on charge, and waved towards the darkened balcony. 'But whoever it is, they must be out there somewhere.'

'Wrap up well,' said Doucette in a resigned tone of voice. 'The nights are still cold.'

Slipping out of the room, she returned a moment later armed with his coat and scarf and a piece of paper.

'Véronique said you know her address, but she gave me the entry code.'

'I'm sorry, Couscous,' said Monsieur Pamplemousse, kissing her goodbye. 'It is good to be home, but perhaps you could ring her and say I am on my way.'

'Take care...'

'I happen to think *Le Guide* is worth preserving,' said Monsieur Pamplemousse simply. 'Come what may.'

'Even though you are no longer working for it?'

Monsieur Pamplemousse nodded.

'I suppose that is one of the reasons why I married you,' sighed Doucette.

'And I thought it was for my looks and my money.'

'One out of three isn't bad,' said Doucette, doing up the top button of the overcoat. 'Will you be taking you know who?'

Monsieur Pamplemousse hesitated. Glancing down, he saw a pair of enquiring eyes. While his wife's back was turned he gave a brief nod in her direction and in return received the canine equivalent of '*d'accord*'.

Given that he had already done enough driving for one day, he set off on foot rather than take his car. As he left the apartment block he gave a quick look round the immediate area, before turning sharp right.

In direct contrast to the southern slopes of Montmartre, where everything went on far into the early hours, the northern side of the Butte was usually deserted at night and the news that some unnamed person had been enquiring after his whereabouts was unsettling to say the least.

Whoever coined the phrase 'the dark is light enough' must have been an incurable romantic. Romantic it might be in the right company. Reassuring it was not.

Reaching a flight of stone steps leading down to the rue Caulaincourt, he thought he heard the sound of footsteps coming from an alleyway running alongside the deserted boules park to his left.

A little voice inside him having whispered 'watch it, Pamplemousse', he waited in the shadows for a moment or two before deciding he must have been mistaken.

Part of him regretted leaving Pommes Frites behind, but in the circumstances he felt it was the right decision. There was also the fact that anyone in the know would automatically associate the one with the other; whenever either one of them appeared on the scene, the other wouldn't be far away. One couldn't be too careful.

Carrying on down the steps, he reached rue Caulaincourt just in time to see the tail lights of an 80 bus disappearing up the road to his left.

Given it would be a good ten minutes or so before the next

one arrived, he was on the point of crossing the road with a view to taking the Metro when he saw a taxi pulling away from the traffic lights.

Flagging it down, he was about to climb in when he heard the sound of a car engine starting up. Glancing across the small square he saw the headlights of what looked like a dark coloured Renault Megane come on.

'Follow the 80 bus,' he said to his driver. '*Vite!*'

The driver gave a grunt as they moved off.

Taking a closer look at the back of the man's head, Monsieur Pamplemousse realised he could be up against a language problem. It was a sign of the times. Taxi drivers not only acted as a barometer to the state of things generally, they also reflected what was happening in far-flung parts of the world. At the time of the Russian revolution Parisian cab drivers had mostly been aristocrats escaping the mob. Now it was refugees from Vietnam and Cambodia or some other war-torn remnant of the French Empire.

Reaching into a hip pocket, he withdrew his credit card wallet, flipped it open momentarily and held it up to the rearview mirror. 'Police!'

The effect was instantaneous. He felt the kick in his back from the Merc's engine as the driver put his foot down. By the time they reached the outskirts of Montmartre cemetery they had caught up with the bus and had to wait their turn at the traffic lights.

Wondering if he had done the right thing after all, he peered out through the back window and, seeing the Renault just breasting the top of the hill and coming up fast behind them, Monsieur Pamplemousse decided to keep his options open for the time being.

The Place Clichy – busy as ever, bright lights, flashing neon signs, crowds queuing for the cinemas – was awash with traffic going in all directions. Fearing his driver might obey instructions to the letter and tuck the car in behind the bus, he instructed the man to carry on, rattling off the route from memory, making doubly sure the message had gone home.

'When you get to the Avenue de la Motte-Picquet, turn right,' he said finally. 'I will tell you when to stop...'

As the lights changed and they accelerated down the relative gloom of the rue de Léningrad, he sank back into his seat, content for the moment to leave matters to the man at the wheel and the good offices of Monsieur Fiacre, Irish hermit and patron saint of taxi-drivers. The big plus, of course, was the fact that by following the same path as the 80 they could make use of bus lanes for much of the way.

He found himself slipping out of one role and into another; from an inspector working for *Le Guide*, back in time to the days when he was an inspector in the Paris *Sûreté*. In truth, he was beginning to enjoy himself.

Gare St Lazare came and went. For once, traffic along both the Boulevard Haussmann and the Avenue Matignon was minimal, but Place de l'Alma was the usual sea of cars and buses entering it and leaving from every possible direction.

There was no sign of the Renault. Which didn't mean it wasn't there; cars were jockeying for position all around them. His driver wriggled through it with masterly aplomb and more than made up for the delay by once again making use of the bus lane operating against the normal flow of traffic in the rue Bosquet.

Two stops along the Avenue de la Motte-Picquet, past the vast École Militaire, they reached a junction where the bus turned left, and he signalled the driver to stop.

It was tempting to tell him to send the bill to the Quai des Orfèvres, which he would have done in the old days, but as the interior light came on, he caught sight of a photograph of two small children attached to the dashboard.

'Yours?'

The driver nodded, his face full of pride. 'They will be excited when I tell them about tonight.'

Monsieur Pamplemousse hastily changed his mind, adding a handsome tip for good measure before he was asked for his autograph.

As the car sped off into the night, he crossed over to the Metro station, took the escalator up to the first level, then made his way up a flight of steps to await the next train to Étoile.

The platform was deserted and nobody else put in an appearance before one arrived. So far, so good.

It was a long time since he had travelled on the elevated line 6. It wasn't simply another view of Paris; at night it was a series of glimpses into other people's lives; a voyeuristic pleasure not unlike a series of disconnected soap operas. Shadowy figures flitted to and fro, or sat at table, sometimes singly, but mostly in pairs or small groups, eating and drinking, watching the 'real thing' on their television screens.

In all probability, behind other windows with closed shutters, all manner of minor dramas were being played out; couples making love, arguing, putting children to bed...or in some cases, coming to terms with old age and loneliness.

Most of the other passengers in his carriage, who probably did the journey every day of their lives, carried on reading their books.

An illuminated poster advertising someone's latest single – 'Every day I love you less and less' came and went. Then the vast shape of the Eiffel Tower loomed into view as they crossed the river by the Pont de Bir Hakeim and, as luck would have it, came alight for its nightly on-the-hour display of pyrotechnics, like some giant firework throwing sparks in all directions.

Realising he had totally lost all track of time, he glanced down at his wrist, only to discover his watch was missing.

He could have sworn he had been wearing it when he left the taxi. Looking around the floor of the carriage, he drew a blank. It must have happened somewhere before boarding the train. If that were the case the chances of finding it would be zero.

Seeing the look of consternation on his face, a woman across the aisle volunteered the fact that it was ten o'clock.

Monsieur Pamplemousse thanked her, but he was inwardly shattered. It was like losing an old friend and he felt bereft, as though something irreplaceable had gone out of his life.

He alighted at the first stop on the far side of the Seine, before the train plunged into the Passy tunnel. Faced with a choice of exits: an escalator leading up to Passy itself, or down a long flight of steps leading to the rue de l'Alboni and the river, he chose the latter. If people were interested in his movements, the last thing he wanted was for them to connect him with the Director's secretary. Call it a belt and braces approach, but that was the way he had been taught, and old habits died hard.

Bernard would have been pleased. According to him, it was on the first floor of No. 1 rue de l'Alboni that Marlon Brando and Maria Schneider memorably discovered a novel use for margarine while filming *Last Tango in Paris*.

Below him, he could hear the endless roar of traffic alongside the river, but once again, there was hardly anyone around. Climbing a flight of stone steps, he made his way along a wide walkway immediately below the Metro line he had just travelled on.

Halfway across the bridge he waited for a gap in the traffic and made for yet another flight of steps, this time leading down to Allée des Cygnes, the man-made island linking it with the Pont de Grenelle further downstream.

During the summer months, when the trees lining either side of the central pathway were in full leaf, it made for a pleasant stroll on a sunny afternoon. On a dark winter's night, with the wind blowing off the river, it felt as cold as charity. He was glad he'd heeded Doucette's advice and worn a scarf.

The walk suited him, though. It helped clear his mind.

It wasn't the first time he had found himself out of a job. The previous occasion had also been the result of a set-up. Allegations regarding some girls at the Folies-Bergère at a time when the police were themselves being investigated had resulted in his taking early retirement from the *Sûreté*.

And yet…in life there are moments when things can seem unutterably bleak, then you turn a corner and suddenly all is sunshine again. It had been that way with *Le Guide*. Just when it seemed as though his life lay in ruins about his feet, a chance meeting with Monsieur Leclercq had provided a golden opportunity to start a new career. Because of his special knowledge and past experience with the food squad, the association had proved invaluable over the years, whenever either *Le Guide*, or the Director himself had been in trouble. The thought that it had now come to an end through no fault of his own was something he had yet to come to terms with.

But if it were another set-up – and he could think of no other word for it – who could have taken the picture? And why? Was there someone out there who had it in for him personally, or was it yet another way of getting at *Le Guide*? Whoever it was, they must have access to inside knowledge.

A Bâteau-Mouche crowded with diners swept past him at speed. From a distance it all looked very romantic; each of its many tables lit by a solitary red shaded lamp, the rest shrouded in a darkness broken only by white-jacketed waiters flitting to and fro. He hoped the food and wine lived up to the setting. For many it would be a night to remember.

Talking of which...he quickened his step. If the Director's secretary was sending out a call for help – and that's what it sounded like – it must be something serious.

In all the years he had been with *Le Guide* he had never known Véronique lose her cool. In many ways she reminded him of Miss Moneypenny in the James Bond films; efficient, imperturbable, tantalisingly self-contained, and sexy with it; almost too good to be true, one might say.

Boulet, ex-wine journal correspondent and *Le Guide's* most recent recruit, had made a bee-line for her on his arrival, and having been rebuffed in no uncertain manner, spread the rumour that she must be a lesbian. But that was only pique, and no one really believed it anyway.

He glanced across the river. The vast apartment blocks adjacent to the Radio France complex looked too snooty for words. He was glad she didn't live there. The older ones he was heading for looked much more inviting.

The fact that Véronique lived in the chic 16th

arrondissement of Paris at all must have appealed to the Director when she first joined him. Monsieur Leclercq set great store by such things.

He had to admit to feeling slightly envious himself. There was something about living near water that appealed to him. After Montmartre, it was like being in the middle of the country. Ignored by guide books, the 16th tended to be patronised by the more intellectual tourists.

If it wasn't film buffs looking for the site of *Last Tango in Paris*, it would be others searching for Balzac's old house. Poor old Balzac, up to his eyes in debt, living there under the assumed name of M. de Brugnal as he worked on *La Comédie Humaine*. Nowadays people were more interested in seeing his coffee pot and photographs of his *amour*, the Comtesse Hanska, than they were reading the novels he had slaved over.

The thought reminded him of the last time he had spent any time in the area.

Curiously enough, it was when *Le Guide* had been under a previous attack. On that occasion, the crime had involved someone hacking into their brand new computer, reprogramming its selection for the Restaurant of the Year and the supreme accolade of a Golden Stock Pot Lid.

He could still remember the look on the Director's face when he ceremonially pressed the button and the words Wun Pooh appeared on the printout; although that was nothing compared to the moment when research revealed it was a Chinese takeaway in Dieppe.

Monsieur Leclercq had inveigled him into assuming the temporary title Head of Security, and since his knowledge of computers at the time could have been written on the back of a postage stamp he had sought the aid of an expert in the field.

He wondered if Martine Borel still lived in her flat overlooking the ivy-covered walls of the rue Berton, Balzac's escape route from his many creditors. He somehow doubted it. She was a high flier and the computer industry changed more rapidly than most.

A second Bâteau-Mouche overtook him, this time it was armed with a battery of floodlights, illuminating the passing scene on both sides of the river. For a mercifully brief moment he was bathed in light as it swept past. So much for keeping a low profile. It left him feeling as naked as the day he was born.

Cameras belonging to a few hardy souls on the top deck flashed as it approached Auguste Bartholdi's original model for the American Statue of Liberty, on the furthermost tip of the Allée.

One last set of steps, this time leading up to the Pont de Grenelle, and he was heading back for the Right bank. He knew he must be getting close because Véronique often spoke of the view of the statue she had from her top floor apartment on the Quai Louis Blèriot.

He wondered what it would be like. Tidy? Almost certainly, if her office was anything to go by. But would it reveal many clues to her life outside the office? Somehow, he doubted it.

For all he knew she might be married, or have a live-in lover. Perhaps even an elderly mother she was looking after. For no particular reason he could put his finger on, none of them seemed to fit the bill.

There was one sure way of finding out. Arriving outside her block a few minutes later, he programmed in the entry code, entered a small hallway, pressed another button for her apartment, and waited for a response. It came almost immediately.

One question was answered soon after the lift arrived at the top floor. Chic as ever in a beige cashmere roll-neck sweater and matching skirt, Véronique volunteered the information almost in the way of an apology as she helped him off with his coat. He couldn't help thinking that when her parents died they must not only have left her the apartment, but the means to carry on living in a style to which she had clearly become accustomed.

'No Pommes Frites?' She looked disappointed.

Monsieur Pamplemousse shook his head. 'He is on an important mission.'

He glanced round as she ushered him into the main living area. The furnishings were much as he had anticipated; a mixture of old and new. He guessed she must have been gradually updating it since her inheritance; quiet, good taste summed it up. Modern, but nothing too way out, and certainly little in the way of photographs or other personal items to give much of a clue as to who lived there. Perhaps such information would be found among the many books occupying shelves lining the far wall to his left.

Below the long picture window, a glass-topped table was home to an old-fashioned gilded birdcage. It looked slightly familiar, yet somehow out of keeping with the rest of the furnishings.

'*Comment allez-vous? Comment allez-vous?*' A gruff voice came from the sole occupant of the cage. Tiny tinkles from a small bell punctuated the words, at the same time ringing a much larger one in his own head.

Raising an eyebrow, he glanced back at Véronique, wondering what on earth Madame Grante's pet budgerigar was doing in her apartment.

Jo Jo had learnt some new words since they last met. Then it had been '*comment ça va?*', but he'd always had trouble with his cedillas. His '*comment allez-vous?*' was infinitely more successful.

However, that was largely academic. Where, he wondered, was Jo Jo's owner when she was at home?

CHAPTER FIVE

Monsieur Pamplemousse's unspoken question received a swift and conclusive response from an unimpeachable source.

Ensconced in a chrome and leather armchair by the window, *Le Guide*'s Head of Accounts clearly enjoyed the look of surprise on his face as she swung round to face him.

'It's confession time,' said Véronique. 'But first things first...'

Motioning him towards a matching chair on the opposite end of the window, she crossed to a table just inside the door, removed an already opened bottle of white wine from a cooler, and began pouring a glass for her guest.

Monsieur Pamplemousse noticed a bowl of water on the floor between the two chairs, presumably in readiness for Pommes Frites; a pointer to the fact that he might be in for a longer session than he had bargained for.

Wilting in the face of Madame Grante's gimlet stare, he began to wish he had taken time to change his clothing and freshen up before setting out. He hadn't even bothered to shave before leaving home. Without feeling his chin, he was suddenly acutely aware of five a.m. stubble.

'Please forgive me,' he began, 'I hadn't planned…'

'It is said that God smiles when he looks down on people and sees them making plans,' said Madame Grante.

So speaks the typical Arien, thought Monsieur Pamplemousse.

In his inimitable way, Bernard had put his finger on it. Having spent time in the wine trade before becoming an inspector, he had a habit of equating people with olive oil.

Véronique, for example, he classed as being *extra-virgine*; flavoursome, with very low acidity and easily digested. Few, apart from the new arrival, Boulet, would have disagreed with his findings. Madame Grante, on the other hand, came under the heading of plain *virgine*. According to Bernard, although often possessed of potentially good flavour, it could also have double the acidity, occasionally causing it to sink to the level of refined oil, thus rendering it basically unsuitable for human consumption.

Monsieur Pamplemousse wondered which it would be tonight. With *Le Guide*'s Head of Accounts it was a case of 'what you saw was what you got'. Viewing the rigid, upright stance and the straight line of her lips set in the thinnest of wintry smiles, he feared the worst.

Her words were probably meant to put him at his ease, but they had quite the opposite effect.

'There must be times,' he said, essaying a second attempt at breaking the ice, 'when God gazes down on the world and wonders if He did the right thing in bringing it all about.'

It was like water off a duck's back.

'Coming events cast their shadows before,' said Madame Grante, in a voice of doom.

Monsieur Pamplemousse reached for his mobile. 'If you will excuse me, I promised to telephone my wife to let her know I am here.'

Although he knew in his heart he was clutching at straws, he also wanted to tell her about the loss of his watch in case he had left it behind, but the thought was still-born.

His sudden movement set off a chain reaction; a piercing shriek, which in turn triggered off the key finder in his jacket pocket.

There was a momentary flash of blue from Jo Jo's cage as he clung to the side of it in order to launch a sustained attack on something pink attached to the bars. The grinding noise only added to the general clamour.

'He always goes straight for his iodised nibble when he is frightened,' said Madame Grante accusingly. 'It comforts him.'

'Perhaps we should all have one,' said Monsieur Pamplemousse, shelving the idea of phoning Doucette for the time being. 'An industrial-size nibble for three, perhaps?'

'*Comment allez-vous?*' Jo Jo reverted to his gruff voice, '*Comment allez-vous?*'

Ask me again in an hour's time, was Monsieur Pamplemousse's gut reaction, but he kept the thought to himself.

Madame Grante picked up her half-empty glass with one hand and Jo Jo's cage with the other. 'I shall leave you in peace,' she said. 'I know you have much to discuss.'

'She's a funny old thing,' said Véronique, handing him the glass of wine when they were alone. 'But she means well and she has a lot on her mind at the moment. Anyway, you looked worried when you arrived, Aristide. Is everything all right?'

Monsieur Pamplemousse told her about his latest loss. 'First my pen, now my watch...I feel bereft without them.'

'*Un malheur n'arrive jamais seul*,' said Véronique.

He gave a shrug. She was right, of course. Misfortunes never seemed to arrive singly.

Véronique seated herself in the chair Madame Grante had vacated. 'Now, I suppose you are waiting for the third thing to happen.'

'There would appear to be no shortage of possibilities,' said Monsieur Pamplemousse gloomily.

He sipped his wine. It was a Riesling. Suitably chilled, clean and perfectly balanced; dry, but with a laid-back fruitiness. It provided instant cheer.

'Superb!'

'It is from Weinbach-Faller.' Véronique acknowledged the compliment. 'Madame Faller brings a woman's touch to wine making.'

'Tell me...' ignoring the temptation to say Heaven forbid Madame Grante should ever take up wine making; acidic levels would be high, he lowered his voice. 'If it isn't a rude question, why is...'

'...Violaine staying with me? Promise you will keep it a secret.'

'I wouldn't dare do otherwise.'

'It all started with something she read in the horoscope section of *le Parisien* – Mars clashing with Venus, or whatever – I'm not too up on these things. She came to see me soon after she began receiving threats and she has been here ever since.'

'Someone has been threatening Madame Grante?' It was hard to picture.

'Not directly…but Jo Jo. In her eyes, that is much, much worse.'

'Jo Jo? What can you possibly threaten a budgerigar with?' asked Monsieur Pamplemousse. 'Other than cutting off its supply of seeds?'

'Dipping its millet spray in prussic acid,' said Véronique. 'Spreading glue on the inside of its bell, ready for when he puts his head under it first thing in the morning. Left there for any length of time it could go rock solid.

'Stapling his little legs together before dropping him out of the window and counting the seconds before he hits the ground.

'Bending his beak back on itself with some hot pliers so that when he is let loose he doesn't know whether he is coming or going.'

'You are not serious?'

'Tying a string round his neck and dipping him into a bowl of batter before plunging him into a saucepan full of hot fat…' continued Véronique. 'There is no end of things you can do to a budgerigar if you are so inclined and have a fertile imagination.

'Supposing it were Pommes Frites?' she added, seeing the look on Monsieur Pamplemousse's face.

'I wouldn't like to be the person who tried it on,' he said grimly.

'But, just supposing…apart from administering a good peck, budgerigars aren't like dogs, they don't have much in the way of defences.'

'I don't want to hear any more.'

'Neither does Madame Grante,' said Véronique. 'Is it any wonder she has been having nightmares? That's why I suggested she stay here with me for the time being. It seemed the most sensible thing to do. She has no one else to turn to.'

'Does Monsieur Leclercq know?' asked Monsieur Pamplemousse. 'About the threats to Jo Jo, I mean.'

Véronique shook her head. 'It all began while he was away in New York. The first time was bad enough, but then it became a daily occurrence...with each threat worse than the one before...Besides, he has enough on his plate at the moment.'

'Were these threats made over the phone?'

'They came through the post.'

'Does she still have the letters? It might give some kind of a lead. Handwriting can be a help in building up a character analysis. Besides, they can do wonders these days with DNA.'

Véronique made a face. 'Violaine burnt them all as fast as they came. She said she couldn't bear having them around, and I'm not surprised. But I doubt if it would have helped a lot even if she had kept them. They were put together using words cut from various sources; journals...headlines in *le Parisien*...advertisements.'

Monsieur Pamplemousse felt doubly glad he had taken precautions against his being followed to her apartment.

'Has she been out at all since she arrived?'

'I have told her to stay in for the time being. She has all the food she needs, and plenty of books.

'The suggestion that she might be replaced by a laptop came as the final straw when she got to hear of it. I can't picture her going back to *Le Guide* at all now.'

'Do you think replacing her that way is remotely possible?'

'No one is indispensable,' said Véronique. 'But it would need to be a very powerful laptop, and it would still need someone to operate it…' She tapped her forehead. 'At the end of the day, it still wouldn't be a match for Madame Grante's very own memory bank.'

'I wonder why?' mused Monsieur Pamplemousse.

'Why?'

'Why something like this has happened now of all times? Is it simply another case of dropping a spanner in the works, or is there some other deeper reason?'

'Her absence has certainly had a bad effect on staff morale,' said Véronique, 'but that is only a small part of it. No doubt Monsieur Leclercq has told you about other things that have been going on while you have been away?'

'Some of them,' said Monsieur Pamplemousse carefully, 'but I imagine not all. Did the letters stop arriving after Madame Grante moved out of her own apartment?'

'That's a thought,' said Véronique. 'I'm afraid I don't know. I can go round and check, if you like.'

'I think perhaps I ought to do it,' said Monsieur Pamplemousse. 'Especially in view of all you have said. Someone may be keeping a watch on her building and I wouldn't want them to put two and two together and follow you back.'

'You think that could happen?' Véronique gave an involuntary shiver.

'From all you have told me,' said Monsieur Pamplemousse, 'I think it is more than likely.

'In fact,' he continued, once again wearing his Quai des Orfèvres hat, 'I would go further. I would suggest that while Madame Grante is staying with you she should take every precaution when she is on her own; ignore any unexpected telephone calls, or someone ringing the entry phone.

'If that happens, she should do what Balzac did when he was in hiding – have some kind of code ready. His used to be "Plums are in season".'

'That sounds highly suspicious for a start,' said Véronique. Glancing over her shoulder she lowered her voice and did a passable imitation of Madame Grante's incisive tones.

'Not very suitable for this time of the year.'

'I believe he had an alternative for other occasions,' said Monsieur Pamplemousse. '"I am bringing lace from Belgium" was one.

'Or…we could invent something.' He plucked an idea out of the air. "Have you noticed champagne glasses are taller this year?"'

'Do you think anyone would say a thing like that?' Véronique sounded dubious.

'Doucette does all the time,' said Monsieur Pamplemousse. 'She bought some new ones the other day and she can't fit them into the dishwasher. She thinks the people who make them are in league with the vineyards, who want people to drink more champagne.

'I tell her it is more likely the makers of dishwashers hoping people will update their machines.'

'Ask a silly question,' said Véronique.

'That is really the whole point,' said Monsieur Pamplemousse. 'You need some kind of statement that will stop a person momentarily in their tracks. In Balzac's case it was a matter of playing for time. Time enough for him to escape from his creditors by going out the back door and taking off down the rue Berton. Madame Grante doesn't have that advantage. There is nowhere for her to go. But if she has a mobile it would give her time to call for help.'

'Oh, dear!' Véronique pulled a face. 'What a mess! I feel it is partly my fault, anyway. Which is really why I wanted to see you as soon as possible.'

'Tell me,' said Monsieur Pamplemousse.

Monsieur Lecercq's secretary gazed out of the window at the winking lights on the far side of the river while she gathered her thoughts.

Another late night Bâteau-Mouche appeared. This time it looked only half full, which still wasn't bad for the time of year. Slowing down to take advantage of the width of the river beyond the end of the Allée, the Captain executed an impeccable U-turn, then the boat quickly gathered speed again as it headed back upstream on the far side of the island.

They both watched until it disappeared out of sight towards its starting point near the Pont Neuf.

He turned to Véronique. 'So…?'

'It all sounds a bit silly, but I really have no one else I can talk to in the office. Working on the top floor has its advantages, privileges if you like, but having others to share your problems with is not one of them.'

'I am honoured,' said Monsieur Pamplemousse. 'But why me?'

'Because of your background,' said Véronique. 'Your time in the *Sûreté*. And most of all because of the fact that although you have always enjoyed a special relationship with Monsieur Leclercq, you have never taken advantage of it. Rather the reverse, it has always seemed to me.'

'I owe it to him,' said Monsieur Pamplemousse simply.

'You may have noticed,' continued Véronique, 'that just lately he has been on one of his periodic belt-tightening missions.'

'I've seen the memos about making sure lights are turned off when you leave a room at night, if that's what you mean,' said Monsieur Pamplemousse.

Véronique got up from her chair and returned with the wine bottle.

'The cost of producing *Le Guide* goes up all the time,' she said, replenishing their glasses. 'As does everything else, of course, but it is a constant worry. The business of Michelin having to pulp their guide to Belgium bothered him more than he was prepared to admit at the time. It was a warning about how vulnerable we are.

'Monsieur Leclercq has steadfastly refused to take advertising. To him that would be the beginning of the end. Also he feels increasing the price is not an option.

'Then there is the constant problem of trying to keep up with current trends in the industry. It is a nightmare. When I first joined *Le Guide*, things evolved slowly. Most chefs stayed where they were for years on end. But the pace of life has hotted up. Nothing stands still any more. People want something new all the time.

'Some of them have lost sight of the fact that the true definition of the word *restaurateur* is one who restores, just as the word *restaurant* itself was originally a medical term. In the beginning it usually meant some form of bouillon-based broth that acted as a restorative.

'Fashions come, and by the time a new edition is ready for publication they are often gone again. There was a time when kiwi fruit was all the rage. Then it was sun-dried tomatoes. Then, when growers couldn't find enough sunshine they became sun-blushed. For a while, *fusion* was the "in" word, along with "froth" and "cappuccino".

'Ingredients that many people had never heard of, like lemongrass and tamarind, suddenly became the "in" words. I read the other day of a chef who has stopped dusting his jellies with powdered sugar but insists on using bee's pollen from the Ba Va mountains in Vietnam.

'Even the language of cooking changes. No one spoons sauce onto a plate any more; they drizzle it.

'Translations are another headache. Going through some press cuttings the other day I came across the word "heretical" being used to describe a piece of cheesecake. There is an English food writer who often makes use of the word "historic" to describe a quite ordinary dish. Americans are fond of the word "revelatory", and they talk of "signature dishes".

'More and more top chefs are spreading their talents too. Nobody expects them to be slaving away over a hot stove all the time – that would be unrealistic, and their great gift to us all is training others up to their standards – but patrons also appreciate continuity and it would be nice if they could show their faces from time to time other than in a fashion magazine.

'In order to keep pace with rising costs, many of the three Stock Pot restaurants in Paris are opening more modestly priced off-shoots nearby; the Bistro Opposite; the Bistro Alongside; the Bistro Two Doors Down. Even Taillevant has branched out with L'Angle, although that is discreetly further away from its parent than most, and stands on its own two feet. Gagnaire has done the same. But chefs can't be in two places at once.

'Cooking is an inexact science, if you choose to call it a science, because you can record all the ingredients, and the times, but you omit the most important one of all: the chef. How can you explain a Bocuse, or a Robuchon or a Gagnaire to the layman? Others can follow their recipes slavishly, but they seldom taste the same.'

Monsieur Pamplemousse had to agree. At the end of the day, the hand that held the ladle was all important. That, along with precision and attention to detail.

Hadn't he once been dining at Paul Bocuse? And hadn't the great man himself, on passing a chicken he had ordered that was turning on a spit in the open fireplace, paused to make some minor adjustment? And hadn't it turned out to be one of the best he had ever eaten? The skin, crisp and golden; the flesh firm and juicy; the taste sublime?

Was it fact or was it fancy? It had certainly made all the difference to his enjoyment of the meal.

It had also pointed the way to a lasting interest in all things to do with food and wine.

'There you are,' said Véronique, when he told her. 'But then Bocuse has the passion.

'Sometimes I wonder where it will all end. Most people have no idea how much work is involved in producing a guide.'

Monsieur Pamplemousse wondered too. Véronique spoke with authority and with passion too, and for perhaps the first time he realised just what an asset she must be to Monsieur Leclercq.

'It is not entirely the fault of the guides,' he said. 'They can only report what they find. We live in an age when the curse of the Top Ten or Top Twenty is upon us. That, and everyone wanting to be a "celebrity".'

'I'm sorry.' Véronique replenished their glasses and then

crossed the room to put the bottle back in its cooler. 'You know all this much better than I do anyway, and it sounds as though I am trying to justify myself, but I did what I did with the best of intentions.'

'So what happened that was so bad?' asked Monsieur Pamplemousse. 'I'm sure it can be put right, whatever it is.'

'I'm afraid it is too late,' said Véronique. 'There is no going back.

'In a way, Madame Grante put the idea into my head. She pointed out to Monsieur Leclercq that his latest trip to America would be the third visit this year, and that fares were going up all the time. She even suggested he might travel tourist class for a change – you can imagine how that went down.

'Consequently, he was in two minds about whether to go or not. Personally, I felt the change of scene might do him good. Also, he needed a break before getting down to serious work on next year's edition.

'What clinched it for me was a piece of junk mail that came through on the office fax machine. These things usually get binned, but it was from a company I hadn't heard of before and the layout happened to be particularly eye-catching. They said they were specialising in first class air and sea fares, and as an opening offer to potential customers they were offering cut-price seats at over sixty per cent off the normal price; twice as much as we normally get.

'Monsieur Leclercq always left his travel arrangements to me, but in the end I asked him what he thought about giving them a trial. His immediate reaction was go for it, provided of course, he was accorded his usual seating arrangements.'

'So, in effect,' said Monsieur Pamplemousse, 'he has only himself to blame.'

Véronique made a face. 'You could say that, but the truth of the matter is, I put the idea into his head in the first place, and since his return he has been a changed person. Something happened while he was away and I feel largely responsible.'

Monsieur Pamplemousse felt half tempted to tell her, but… Once again he automatically looked for his watch, then made do with a large clock on one of the walls.

It was getting late and his mind was in too much of a whirl as it was. It was hard to equate the Director's encounter on the plane with what was happening back home, but if they were connected, then Monsieur Leclercq must be in worse trouble than he had pictured. Up to his knees, as Bernard might say. He decided to gloss over it for the time being.

'You really shouldn't lose any sleep,' he said. 'I am sure it is a passing storm. It will blow itself out eventually.'

'The way he is behaving is having an effect on everything,' persisted Véronique. 'It is permeating right down through the system. At first it was little things, like pensioning off old Rambaud and bringing in the new man.'

'You don't like the man from BRINKS?'

'Paul Bourdel? Nobody likes him. That was really the start of it all. Now, the entries in *Le Guide* itself are being sabotaged in some way.'

'And the firm who provided the tickets? You have used them again since?'

Véronique shook her head. 'It was a flash in the pan. I tried to get through, but they must have gone under already. Businesses come and go these days. Nothing is for ever.'

'If you let me have the details,' said Monsieur

Pamplemousse, 'I can get someone to check up on them.'

'I don't have them here,' said Véronique. 'Next time you come into the office...'

'I'm afraid that will not be possible.'

'Not possible?'

'Monsieur Leclercq hasn't told you?'

Monsieur Pamplemousse broke off to relate the outcome of his morning visit. In the event, Véronique had been out of her room when he and Pommes Frites left, but he assumed she would have been told on her return.

'The old devil,' she said, when he had finished his tale of woe. 'He didn't say a word about it. Not one word. In fact, it struck me that after your visit he seemed in much better spirits; almost as though a great weight had been lifted from his mind. I actually heard him humming a few bars of "La Donna e Mobile".

'You are not taking it seriously, of course.'

'I can hardly ignore it. Besides, my mind is made up. If Pommes Frites goes, then I go too. There is a principle at stake.'

'I can understand that,' said Véronique. 'But principles don't pay the bills, Aristide. Anyway, surely things said in the heat of the moment...'

'It wasn't exactly the heat of the moment,' said Monsieur Pamplemousse. 'In fact, I remember his words very clearly. Not only that, but I remember the tone in which they were said. He couldn't have spelt them out more clearly.

'When I semi-jokingly asked when would be a good time for me to leave, he looked at his watch and said, quite simply: "I think now is a very good moment, Pamplemousse". It left no room for argument even if I'd had a mind to.

'After all the years I have been with *Le Guide*, we parted company without so much as a handshake. It was not a happy occasion.'

'This is worse than I thought,' said Véronique, 'much worse. Do you think he *is* heading for a nervous breakdown?'

'If he is, I am sorry, but…' Monsieur Pamplemousse gave a noncommittal shrug, hands outspread.

'I do worry about him,' said Véronique, considering the possibility. 'It is always worse at this time of the year. Nothing gives him more pleasure than to see someone being awarded an additional Stock Pot. Conversely, he agonises for days when it is a question of demotion. He worries about the effect it will have, not only on their business but on their personal life as well; their health, their family – the possibility that some will take it so badly it will be the end of everything. I don't know what I would do if that happened.'

'You mean suicide?'

'It happens from time to time,' said Véronique. 'When total depression sets in.'

'But that has always been so,' said Monsieur Pamplemousse. 'We French take the business of food very seriously. Over the years many have become martyrs to the cause of gastronomy.

'Remember Vatel, who stabbed himself to death with a sword over the simple matter of the late arrival of some fish? Only two baskets arrived instead of the vast quantity that was expected for a lunch he was cooking for Louis XIV. He was one of a long line who have died in the cause of gastronomy. It comes under the heading of failure to uphold the highest traditions of their profession. According to Madame de Sévigné, it quite spoilt the King's party.'

'That was in 1671,' said Véronique, 'and Louis XIV did have an entourage of several hundred. It wasn't as though he was cooking a dinner for two.'

'How about the chef at the Relais de Porquerolles, the one who shot himself after losing his Michelin star?' suggested Monsieur Pamplemousse.

'That was also a long time ago; nearly forty years. I am thinking of more recent events.'

'Bernard Loiseau?'

'That hit Monsieur Leclercq hard. Over the years they had become friends. It was unnecessary, too. There was a rumour of his being downgraded in Gault Millau, but there was no suggestion of him being demoted in *Le Guide* or Michelin.'

'There must have been other reasons,' said Monsieur Pamplemousse. 'Even without him his restaurant still enjoys top rating in all the guides.'

'He was out in the sticks,' said Véronique. 'Following the 2001 terrorist attacks in New York, the number of wealthy Americans flying to Europe dropped alarmingly, and the local trade wasn't sufficient to fill the restaurant during the winter months. Restaurants are like theatres – there is no quicker way of losing money than having them only half full. It had taken him twenty years to build up the business and suddenly it was on the verge of collapse. He also had an enormous loan to pay back. It was as simple as that.

'Anyway, that still doesn't make it any better. And it still doesn't solve *Le Guide*'s present problems. Someone, somehow, is double guessing everything we do, and quietly sabotaging it. If things carry on as they are I can't picture our being able to publish next year's edition and that would be a catastrophe. All our jobs are at risk; our jobs, and all those in the trade who count on receiving a mention.'

'I am hardly in a position to help,' said Monsieur Pamplemousse.

'There is no reason why Monsieur Leclercq should know,' said Véronique.

'And as far as anyone else in the company is concerned, you are still on the staff.'

'I wouldn't know where to begin,' said Monsieur Pamplemousse lamely.

'We think,' said Véronique, 'Monsieur Leclcerq is being ill-advised.'

'We, being...'

'Violaine and myself.' As if he hadn't guessed!

He threw a balloon in the air. 'When you say he is being ill-advised, you mean the new time and motion person? He seems to be rubbing people up the wrong way, right, left and centre.'

'That is one way of putting it. I gather you haven't met.'

'You do not like him either?'

Véronique hesitated. 'I think perhaps you should form your own opinion, and as soon as possible. You could meet outside the office. For dinner perhaps? I can arrange a suitable rendezvous.'

It had taken a roundabout route to reach that point, and it had been dropped into the conversation as though it were a case of sudden inspiration, but it was almost too casual. He would have bet anything it had been planned all along. Véronique was being the soul of discretion as ever.

'Women's intuition?'

'Something like that. And don't forget...there are *two* of us. And don't lose sight of the problem with Jo Jo – while he is still around. It would be nice to keep things the way they are.'

Véronique was right. It might have been Pommes Frites. It could still be, the way things were heading. He knew when he was beaten.

'We must do something about it,' he said.

The communicating door opened and Madame Grante entered the room complete with cage.

'I couldn't help overhearing,' she said, coming towards them. 'You are a very kind man, Monsieur Pamplemousse.'

Clearly, a thaw had set in, and for the briefest of moments he thought she was about to embrace him, cage and all, but once again the sudden movement caught Jo Jo off balance.

'*Bonne journée*,' came a gruff voice. '*Bonne journée.*'

Monsieur Pamplemousse beamed his goodnights towards the speaker. Jo Jo might not be the greatest conversationalist in the world, but give him his due, despite living in a world dominated by millet sprays and iodine nibbles; he did have impeccable timing.

'I will await your call,' he said to Véronique.

CHAPTER SIX

The next day, having taken advantage of his new-found freedom, Monsieur Pamplemousse arrived back rather later than usual from his morning walk with Pommes Frites. He was about to slip his key into the lock on the apartment door, when he paused.

Pommes Frites looked equally surprised when he heard an unexpected voice coming from the other side of it, and he eyed his master quizzically.

'Guess who's here,' said Doucette, as they entered the apartment. 'Madame Leclercq!'

'Please, I must insist,' said the Director's wife, 'do call me Chantal. I know your husband would prefer it that way.'

'It has been a long time,' said Doucette lamely.

'All the more reason not to stand on ceremony, is that not so, Aristide?'

As Monsieur Pamplemousse drew near, Madame Leclercq held out her hand to be kissed. There was a flirtatious side to her that was never far from the surface, especially when she wanted something. Most people put it down to her Italian connections and a reputed early training for the world of opera, although there were those who said the latter was really only singing lessons and the term 'opera' a conceit on the part of her husband.

One thing was certain, the tiny hand Monsieur Pamplemousse encountered with his lips was far from frozen, nor was it withdrawn as quickly as it might have been; something he felt sure his wife could hardly have failed to register.

He wondered what the problem was this time.

'I will go and put the coffee on,' said Doucette tactfully.

'Henri has got himself into a mess.' Madame Leclercq wasted no time in getting down to brass tacks as soon as they were alone.

'Has he really?' said Monsieur Pamplemousse guardedly.

'Either that, or he is having an affair, but somehow I don't think that is the reason. I suspect it has more to do with work; possibly even a mixture of both.'

'It is a busy time of the year,' agreed Monsieur Pamplemousse. 'He has a great many things on his mind.'

Privately he agreed with her analysis. Having married into money, Monsieur Leclercq knew only too well which side of his bread was buttered. That mattered a lot to him. He was hardly likely to risk it all on a brief flirtation.

'It couldn't have come at a worse time,' said Chantal. 'As you know, the local elections are coming up soon and he is in the running for the post of mayor in our village; something he has always coveted. It brings with it so many advantages, but the slightest whiff of scandal before he gets it…'

'Perhaps it is a touch of *le demon de midi*?' suggested Monsieur Pamplemousse.

'I am sure it will all blow over.'

'Men!' said Chantal with feeling. 'They blame everything on the mid-life crisis, as though there is absolutely nothing they can do about it! We women have our problems in that area too, you know.'

Monsieur Pamplemousse remained silent. Madame Leclercq's must have arrived early, for he still remembered the occasion when she had played footsie with him under the table. It was during one of the Director's annual staff parties at their summer residence near Deauville. At least, he had always assumed it was her foot. It had been hard to tell at the time because others had been at it too. In fact, the whole table ended up in a state of chaos following Pommes Frites' discovery, while sitting beneath it, that pressing the odd toe with his paw in order to relieve the boredom produced some unexpected results.

From the way he was behaving now, sniffing Madame Leclercq's bag on the floor beside her chair, it looked as though he might be reliving the occasion.

'What do you make of a husband who returns home with the end of his tie missing?' asked Chantal.

Someone who is asking for trouble, thought Monsieur Pamplemousse. 'Perhaps he shut it in his car door?' he said out loud. 'It is easily done.'

'If you ask me,' said Chantal, 'Henri went to some nightclub or other while he was in New York. No doubt you remember Regine. It was her trademark when she ran a club in Paris. I suspect whoever was responsible must have kept the piece she cut off as a souvenir. It is not in his suitcase.'

'In Germany, during carnival week,' mused Monsieur Pamplemousse, 'I believe women dress up as witches and roam the streets armed with scissors, snipping the end off men's ties. It is a symbolic gesture, which interestingly starts at exactly 11.11 a.m., eleven being the magic carnival number.'

'That takes place in February,' said Chantal. 'Besides, I met Henri at the airport and I know he came off the plane from New York.'

Monsieur Pamplemousse conceded defeat. He had done his best – he couldn't do more.

'What I did come across in his carry-on bag,' continued Chantal, 'was a handkerchief covered in lipstick. It had been stuffed inside a little-used compartment. There was also a membership card for some kind of health club. It sounded very suspect to me.

'And another thing…' Madame Leclercq was in full flight and there was no stopping her. 'Normally, when Henri arrives home after a long trip he takes it easy for the rest of the week, but the very next day he went out early saying he had an urgent appointment, and later that morning I saw him lurking in Dior.

'I happened to be parking my car on the other side of the Avenue Montaigne and he was peering out into the street. By the time I entered the shop he had disappeared. The staff denied all knowledge, of course. No doubt they had been suitably primed, but I know I wasn't seeing things.'

'He could have been looking for a new tie,' said Monsieur Pamplemousse hopefully.

'In the dress department?'

'Christmas isn't so far away,' countered Monsieur Pamplemousse. 'He may have been buying you a present.'

'He could have done that while he was in New York,' said Chantal.

'And that's another thing...something happened on the return flight.'

'It did?' said Monsieur Pamplemousse. Endeavouring to inject a suitable note of surprise into his voice it came out rather higher pitched than he had intended.

'In my experience,' continued Chantal, 'there is only one thing more calculated to arouse a wife's suspicions than having her husband ring up out of the blue from the middle of the Atlantic Ocean to tell her there is absolutely nothing to worry about...'

Monsieur Pamplemousse pricked up his ears. One learnt something new every day. 'Tell me,' he said.

'That is when he pretends to be an American businessman who is having trouble with his daughter and has got the wrong number,' said Chantal. 'Henri may fancy himself as an actor, but I would know his voice anywhere.

'He even had the gall to suggest we meet up while he was in Paris. Naturally, I said "yes". I thought it might teach him a lesson. Besides, I knew he wasn't in a position to carry it through.'

'Perhaps it was some kind of game,' suggested Monsieur Pamplemousse.

'If that were so,' said Chantal, 'it certainly took the airline in. A large bouquet of flowers arrived yesterday morning, along with a letter of apology. It was addressed to *Mademoiselle* Leclercq, suggesting that if she cared to submit a bill from the cleaners it would be taken care of. They sincerely hoped she would fly with them again in the very near future. Can you explain that?'

Monsieur Pamplemousse could have, but he didn't. He waited instead.

'Henri has been behaving very strangely ever since he got back,' said Chantal. 'Usually, when he returns from America he is full of the latest jargon. He can't wait to pepper his speech with what he thinks are the latest Americanisms: hostile environment, fast track, synergy, bottom line, revisit, leverage, game plan, back boiler…Usually, by the time he arrives home they are already *passé*, and in this instance doubly so because he had already used most of them up over the telephone.'

Monsieur Pamplemousse sat down beside her. 'I have no doubt there is a simple explanation.'

'Do you really think so?' Chantal rested a hand on his for a moment, her blue eyes full of hope. 'I am so worried.'

'I am certain of it.'

'The problem is,' she said slowly, 'my Uncle Caputo. You know what he is like.'

Monsieur Pamplemousse gave a start. Having had dealings with Madame Leclercq's Sicilian uncle in the past, he did indeed know what he was like. His real name was Rocco and he hadn't acquired the nickname Caputo for nothing. His Mafia connections were common knowledge.

'Surely, there is no reason why he should know. Whatever transpired, it can hardly be headline news.'

'That is just the trouble,' said Chantal. 'It is really why I came to see you, Aristide. I trust I may call you Aristide?' She gave his hand a squeeze. 'You see, he rang up out of the blue yesterday evening and asked if all was well between Henri and myself.

'It seems a business friend of his, who runs a chain of mobile laundries in Palermo, was travelling on the same plane and witnessed some kind of encounter between my husband

and a young nun who was sitting next to him. Uncle Caputo's friend has connections with financial circles in the Vatican and they were appalled by the news. To make matters worse, he also reported back that he heard Henri trying to make a date with someone.'

Reminded of the Director's comment about the kind of people one met when travelling first class, Monsieur Pamplemousse couldn't help but give a wry smile.

'I am Uncle Caputo's favourite niece,' continued Chantal, 'and he told me he didn't know what he would do if anything went wrong with our marriage. Reading between the lines, I think he knows exactly what he would do, and it wouldn't be very pleasant. Henri would have more than the end of his tie cut off. And that would only be the beginning.

'I am so worried for him. I know Uncle Caputo. Once he has made up his mind to do something, that is it. He is a man of his word. To go back on it would be to lose respect. In his position he cannot afford to make allowances for the frailties of others.'

'It is all very unfortunate,' began Monsieur Pamplemousse, 'but I am not sure how I can help...'

'He hopes you will do something about it. He said he knew you wouldn't let him down.'

'Me?' Monsieur Pamplemousse sat up. 'Why me?'

'He thinks very highly of you,' said Chantal. 'That has been so ever since the time you saved his daughter from a fate worse than death. If you remember, you acted as her escort when she came to Paris by train that time.'

With the avowed intention of opening a brothel, thought Monsieur Pamplemousse. No sooner had the night express from Rome arrived at the Gare de Lyon than she disappeared.

It had turned out well in the end, but for a while his life had been teetering on a knife edge. He wouldn't want to risk a repeat performance.

'A lovely girl,' he said. 'So like her father, even though she was still at school.'

'I don't know what I would do if anything happened to Henri,' said Chantal simply. 'He means the world to me.'

Suddenly reaching across, she threw her arms around Monsieur Pamplemousse.

Enveloping him in a cloud of heady perfume, she pressed her bosom against his and began to cry.

'Before he hung up,' she said between sobs, 'Uncle Caputo asked me what size shoes Henri wears. We all know what that means...'

Monsieur Pamplemousse was too much of a gentleman to put it into words, but phrases like 'concrete boots' and 'bottom of the Seine' immediately sprang to mind.

'He specifically mentioned the Canal St Martin,' said Chantal, reading his mind.

'He looks on it as doing me a favour. He kept saying things like "You are one of the *famiglia*, Chantal. It is all for the best".

'You *must* help me, Aristide. Please, I beg of you...I feel so frightened and alone and I have no one else to turn to...'

With the best will in the world, Monsieur Pamplemousse found it hard to avoid feeling his stomach turning to water. He was dimly aware of the fact that somewhere in their apartment a phone was ringing, but escape was impossible. A tear landing on his cheek rolled unchecked onto his shirt. He pictured the trail of mascara it must have left in its wake. Doucette would not be pleased.

Instinctively reaching down to his trouser pocket for a handkerchief, he encountered a hand. It was even warmer than it had been the first time, and he was about to withdraw his own for fear his action might be misconstrued, when it was caught in a vice-like grip.

'I forget,' said Doucette sweetly, as she came back into the room carrying a tray. 'Do you take milk with your coffee?'

'Trouble, Aristide?' she asked, as soon as Chantal had departed. 'I couldn't help overhearing some of it.'

'You could say, Couscous, I was saved by the proverbial bell.'

Straightening the cushions, Doucette sniffed the air. 'Eau d'Hadrien from Annick Goutal.

'I asked her,' she said, seeing her husband's look of surprise. 'It is said to be very seductive. No wonder you were in need of being rescued.'

'Italians dramatise everything,' said Monsieur Pamplemousse. 'It is in their blood. Monsieur Leclercq is potentially in much deeper water than I am.'

He must also have been skating on thinner ice than he realised during his shopping tour with Maria. Had they met up in Annick Goutal, for example, Chantal might have rendered her uncle's services null and void on the spot.

'And you intend going to his aid?'

'Looking at the whole matter realistically,' said Monsieur Pamplemousse, 'I don't really have much choice. There is an old saying. "Once a policeman..."'

'"...always a policeman".' Doucette finished the sentence for him.

'The words are as true today, Couscous,' said Monsieur Pamplemousse, 'as when they were first uttered.'

'I know,' sighed Doucette, 'but if I have said it once, Aristide, I have said it a hundred times. I did think when you went to work for a food guide it would be the end of my worries. Instead of which...'

'It won't be for long,' said Monsieur Pamplemousse optimistically. 'In the meantime, perhaps we can go out this evening and make the most of my being at home...' Catching the look on her face, he broke off. 'No?'

'Véronique phoned while you were otherwise engaged,' said Doucette. 'She has made a reservation for you tonight at Lapérouse.' She took a closer look. 'I think you had better change your shirt before you go anywhere.'

'Lapérouse? Are you sure?' It didn't sound like Véronique.

'Positive. Eight o'clock. She said it is in your name, but not to worry; the bill will be taken care of. She also made the point that it wasn't her choice and suggested you take Pommes Frites with you.'

Monsieur Pamplemousse looked dubious.

'It's all right for some,' said Doucette.

'I was thinking I would rather he stayed at home,' said Monsieur Pamplemousse. 'I don't like leaving you on your own.'

'I haven't been to Lapérouse since that time you took me soon after we met,' said Doucette dreamily. 'I remember it all so clearly; the mirrors and the decorated ceilings, the panelling, the candlelight...most of all the candlelight. It was all very romantic, or so it seemed at the time.

'All my friends teased me and suggested you were planning to seduce me in one of their *petits salons discret*; the ones with just room for two and a bell to let the waiter know when it is safe to enter.'

'Were you very disappointed finding yourself in one of the main rooms, Couscous?'

'You will never know,' said Doucette.

'It cost me an arm and a leg as it was, without having to leave an extra tip for the waiter to ignore the bell if it rang more than once.'

Doucette blushed. 'I wonder if it is still the same?'

'Apart from the candlelight, I doubt if it has changed since Victor Hugo used to take his children there,' said Monsieur Pamplemousse. 'Timelessness is what restaurants like Lapérouse are all about.'

'I really meant the private rooms,' said Doucette.

'As far as I know there are some still left – the "Salon des Anges" and "La Belle Otéro", but I certainly don't intend finding out, if that's what you mean.'

'We had *Poulet Docteur*,' said Doucette. 'You told me Georges Simenon once used the setting for a Maigret story and the dish was named after that gourmet doctor friend of his in the books, although I have since heard it said the food is not like it was then.'

'It has had its ups and downs over the years,' admitted Monsieur Pamplemousse. 'But they have a new chef and currently it is on its way up again. At least for once I shan't have to write a report. I can sit back and enjoy the experience.'

'I had better give a certain dog a bath if he's going there,' said Doucette. 'He ought to be looking his best.'

'There is a price to pay for everything in this world,' called Monsieur Pamplemousse, as Pommes Frites, having pretended not to hear, slowly followed his mistress out of the room. He was wearing his gloomy expression.

Left to his own devices, Monsieur Pamplemousse began to wonder why the table had been booked in his name. And why insist on his taking Pommes Frites? Véronique must have her reasons.

For a moment he felt tempted to ring her. Then his thoughts turned to Chantal's visit. Clearly, she had no idea he was now an ex-employee of *Le Guide*, but it was one more item to add to his growing list of interested parties.

The overall problem concerning *Le Guide* certainly wouldn't go away. Véronique's simple plea had gone home. To ignore it would be to go against all that he had held dear during the latter part of his life. The Director's wife apart, there were so many others involved he couldn't let them down.

Reaching for the phone, he dialled a number and waited. Jacques must be out on a job. Normally, his erstwhile colleague from the Paris *Sûreté* days took great pride in answering before the second ring and he was on the point of hanging up when his patience was rewarded.

'I have a favour to ask,' he said, once they were through with the preliminaries.

'Could you possibly find out for me if you have anything on a man by the name of Péage…?'

'When do you need it by?' Jacques sounded harassed.

'In an ideal world,' said Monsieur Pamplemousse. 'As soon as possible, if not before.'

The response was not unexpected.

'Yes, I know you have a lot of paperwork to deal with.'

'The more we get computerised,' said Jacques, 'the more paper we have to deal with. The paperless society is a myth.'

'You think I don't suffer that too?' said Monsieur

Pamplemousse, thinking of all the entries he had to make every time he went on one of his trips.

'I'm afraid I don't have a first name...

'No...nor an address...

'No... I don't have a photograph of him either...'

He held the phone away from his ear.

'Jacques...there *are* no haystacks in Paris... If it were that easy I would do it myself. Besides, it is your turn... Remember the business with Claude Chavignol?'

'Do I ever?' Mention of the apparent demise of France's premier television chat show host before an audience of millions did the trick.

The two of them had been in at the kill, as it were, three if you included Pommes Frites, who had played a vital part in the whole affair.

'I received a mention in dispatches for that,' said Jacques proudly.

'That's more than we did,' said Monsieur Pamplemousse.

'*C'est la vie*,' said Jacques. 'What's it worth?'

'*Dejeuner*...your choice of venue?'

Monsieur Pamplemousse knew the bait wasn't necessary. He also knew Jacques wouldn't take advantage of such an offer, even if he did take it up. As always, it would simply be good to see each other again and catch up on the latest news; reminisce about their times together on the Food Fraud squad, seeking out those suspected of passing-off such things as Chinese truffles for the real thing. There was no end to people's duplicity.

Jacques held a much more exalted position now, but they had never lost touch with each other. He was a true friend. The sort you don't necessarily have to see. It was sufficient to know he was there when needed. No questions asked.

'Anything else while I'm at it?'

Monsieur Pamplemousse threw a balloon into the air.

'What do you think the odds are of the Director sitting next to a nun on a flight back from America? Not only that, but a nun who had been on a similar business seminar to one he had just been attending.'

'I think,' said Jacques, after a moment's pause, 'there are a number of factors involved. They need to be separated before discussing probabilities.

'To start with, I imagine Monsieur Leclercq would be up front rather in the back of the plane. That means he would be travelling with other so-called "high flyers"; professional people who move in similar circles. In which case, the odds would be considerably longer.

'To my mind, a much more realistic approach would be to find out how many nuns are flying worldwide at any given moment – I wouldn't mind betting most of them use Alitalia anyway. They probably get special rates. Secondly, how many of them are likely to be travelling first class. I would stick my neck out and say not many.

'That being so,' he continued, 'what are the chances of their ending up sitting next to the Director?'

'You tell me,' said Monsieur Pamplemousse.

It was like solving a difficult crossword puzzle clue. Reading it out loud suddenly made the answer seem obvious.

'Zilch. *Zéro. Rien de rien.* Unless, of course, it had been fixed in advance.'

'*Exactement!* That would be my guess too.'

'I take it these things are connected,' said Jacques. 'You've got me interested, Aristide. I'll ring you back as soon as possible. You can update me on it all, as and when. Over that lunch perhaps?'

'*Ciao.*' Monsieur Pamplemousse replaced the handset, consulted his notebook again, then picked up the receiver and, on the off-chance, dialled another number. This time he drew a blank.

'Promise you won't answer the door if anyone calls,' he said, when he kissed Doucette goodbye that evening.

'You take good care too,' said Doucette. She slipped a small object into his trouser pocket. 'And while you are there, see if you can take a few pictures for old time's sake. You might not get another chance.'

Feeling in his pocket, Monsieur Pamplemousse recognised the Director's latest toy, a sleek, all-black Leica C-Lux2 digital camera; the latest in a long line of possible replacements for the Leica R4 35-millimetre camera, used for archive recording purposes by staff while on their travels. Apart from the initial expense, it was the latest manifestation of his cost-cutting exercises. The annual saving on film alone would be enormous, but for some years the camera industry had kept one step ahead of him. No sooner had he reached a decision, than something new and better came along.

As had been the case at various times over the years, Monsieur Pamplemousse had been entrusted with delivering a report on its usefulness.

Giving Doucette a final hug, he waited outside the door until he heard the bolt and chain being put into place.

She hadn't meant it that way, but the phrase 'might not get another chance' brought home to him as nothing else would have done the fact that one shouldn't take things for granted. Nothing in this life was for ever. For years now, *Le Guide's* issue case, full of the latest equipment to cope with any emergency, had gone everywhere with him. Now, as soon as he handed the camera in, as hand it in he must, he would become an *ex*-employee, out in the cold, hard world. At least, having refused to part with his old Citroën rather than use a company car, he wouldn't be without transport.

As for the camera; he would have to start getting used to his old Voigtlander again.

The realisation was compounded some twenty minutes or so later when he was leading the way along the Quai des Grands-Augustins. Mulling over the future, he was caught in the momentary glare of a flash gun.

A couple hovering outside Lapérouse were engaged in a slight altercation.

'OK. So, how about *you* taking it next time?' said the woman. 'This camera is so old I'm on my second shoulder strap.'

There was another flash as the man took over.

'*Excusez-moi.*' Monsieur Pamplemousse edged past them and made his way inside, quickly announcing his presence before the couple beat him to it.

Registering the barest flicker of surprise when she saw Pommes Frites, the receptionist took his coat, summoned an underling to relieve her of it and deal with the other new arrivals, then led the way up a flight of stairs.

As they turned the first corner he caught sight of the American woman giving her husband a nudge and, camera raised, pointing towards Pommes Frites. Clearly, her worst fears were about to be realised; or her wildest expectations. Whichever, shoulder strap or no shoulder strap, another photo was added to her store of memories.

Expecting to turn left at the top of the stairs into one of the larger salons facing the Seine, Monsieur Pamplemousse found himself entering a corridor to the right instead.

'The Otéro, monsieur,' said the girl, motioning him through an open door to the first of a series of small rooms. '*Bon appetit.*'

'Are you sure?' asked Monsieur Pamplemousse.

'*Absolument,* monsieur!' Looking as near to being offended as decorum allowed, she signalled their arrival to an assistant *maître d'* hovering nearby. 'I took the booking myself.'

Following them into the room, the man eyed Pommes Frites. 'Would monsieur's guest like still or sparkling water?'

'My dog,' said Monsieur Pamplemousse, 'prefers Chateldon.' He could have added, along with Louis XIV and serious wine tasters everywhere on account of its purity. It was his usual test. A bonus point if they had it, a means of establishing a certain measure of ascendancy at the outset if they didn't.

'Of course, monsieur.'

'My main guest,' said Monsieur Pamplemousse pointedly, 'has yet to arrive.'

'*Oui,* monsieur.' The Assistant *Maître d'*, who looked as though he had seen it all over the years, bowed and withdrew.

Left to his own devices, Monsieur Pamplemousse took out his camera and seized the opportunity to satisfy Doucette's wishes by taking a few pictures for old time's sake; he might not get the chance later.

To say the room was small was putting it mildly. Not surprisingly, Pommes Frites was having trouble finding enough space in which to lie down.

The light from the chandelier wasn't exactly dazzling.

Doucette would have been disappointed with the rather too modern bulbs hanging at a rakish angle. Programming the camera's built-in flash facility, he set to work.

The circular table in the middle, with its two place settings, more than filled the frame.

The upper half of the walls, decorated with ancient *trompe l'oeil* frescoes in the style of Boucher and Watteau, made satisfactory shots, as did the ornamental carvings on the bottom section. To his left, beyond a curtained window, a small chaise longue, the cushions covered in matching deep red velvet, added a welcome touch of colour, but getting a satisfactory shot of the large mirror above it without seeing his own reflection wasn't so easy.

A well-worn brass plate to one side bore the simple inscription 'Curnonsky', making it one of twenty-seven distributed among leading Paris restaurants by fellow gastronomes on the occasion of the self-styled 'Prince of Gastronomes' eightieth birthday. Attached to the best seats, it meant that for the rest of his life he only had to reach for his telephone to be guaranteed a place and a free meal.

He wondered how the author of the 32-volumed *La France Gastronomique* would have viewed Lapérouse now. Chefs had come and gone, but, like the big wheel, as one person alighted another got on. He doubted if the restaurant itself had changed a great deal.

Originally built to serve the needs of chicken farmers in need of somewhere to carry out their business transactions, the rooms must have been equally successful in later years when put to other uses if the scratchings on the mirror were anything to go by.

That said, if it were simply a case of getting to know

someone in peace and quiet, it was tailor made.

Looking round to his right he noticed a plastic bell-push fixed to the wall; presumably to summon a waiter when one was required. Idly wondering if it was functioning, he pressed it.

The door opened almost immediately and a commis waiter appeared with a bowl and a bottle of Chateldon. Having shown Pommes Frites the label, he solemnly decanted it. At the same time, the Assistant *Maître d'* entered with the menu and the wine list.

Declining the offer of an aperitif before his guest arrived, Monsieur Pamplemousse waited until the door was closed before settling down to study what was on offer. There was no harm in being ahead of the game early on.

The fixed-price menu included a reasonable selection for all four courses.

Mentally opting for *l'oeuf Pierrot aux truffes*, whatever that was – the mere mention of truffles did the trick – he decided on a *noix S. Jacques risotto* to follow, and perhaps the Soufflé Lapérouse after the cheese. Doucette was right; he might as well make the most of his opportunities while they lasted.

He knew one thing; having the door closed meant the heat was rapidly becoming more and more oppressive. The sound of lapping suggested Pommes Frites was feeling it too.

Parting the net curtains and feeling a draft of hot air rising from a radiator, he opened the window slightly and, seeing a restaurant on the other side of the road full of diners, automatically took out his camera.

Les Bouquinistes had a good write-up in *Le Guide* and old habits to record such moments died hard. So what if he was taken for a tourist?

Turning back away from the window, he decided to take one last shot of the room.

Flattening himself against the wall, he zoomed out, pressed the shutter release button halfway down to bring the picture into sharp focus, and was about to take a picture of the door, including as much as possible of the gilded surround, when it swung open.

Expecting to see a waiter, the viewing screen was filled instead by an elegant figure that wouldn't have disgraced the front cover of some glossy fashion magazine.

He was about to say there must be some mistake, when he saw the receptionist hovering in the background and hurriedly changed his mind.

The first time he had queried her hadn't gone down too well. Twice might be one too many.

CHAPTER SEVEN

It was hard to say who was the most taken aback; the person standing in the doorway, Monsieur Pamplemousse, or Pommes Frites, who couldn't decide whether to wag his tail or not. In the end he left it at half mast.

During the split second it took the camera to readjust to the change of scene the new arrival paused and smiled directly into the lens.

Monsieur Pamplemousse instinctively zoomed in for a tighter shot. If nothing else, it was a good test of the camera's ability to cope with all eventualities. Almost at once a pin-sharp picture appeared on the screen.

Mentally awarding it ten out of ten, he pressed the shutter-release button fully home and, as he did so, he became aware of something odd about the person's face, but by then it was too late.

The operation completed, he glanced up, and realised what had been bothering him. Although one of the subjects's eyes had been staring straight towards the lens, the other was focused on Pommes Frites.

'*Buonasera, signorita,*' he said. '*Mi chiamo Aristide Pamplemousse. E tu come ti Maria?*'

Monsieur Leclercq was right about one thing: the eye nearest to him immediately lost its sparkle, effectively disposing of the girl's knowledge of Italian and presumably with it, her so-called connections to the Vatican.

'Good evening,' he translated. 'My name is Aristide Pamplemousse, and you must be Maria.'

'How *did* you guess?'

The girl entered the room, and as she turned to close the door he seized the opportunity to carry out a quick survey.

Clearly, he was privileged to be taking part in an early viewing of the fruits of her shopping expedition with Monsieur Leclercq.

The knee-length white satin dress she was wearing would have brought about an impatient snort from Doucette had she come across it in one of her magazines. From the way it clung to her body it might have been made from some form of semi-transparent plastic film, more suited to a hot summer's day on the promenade in Cannes than a winter evening in Paris. If it was 'off the shelf', then it must have been awaiting her arrival, for she filled it to perfection; a walking tribute to the art of haute couture.

A matching handbag and shoes completed the ensemble.

Monsieur Leclercq was right in one respect: the girl could fairly be described as being a pretty little thing, but having said that, his immediate reaction was he wouldn't have trusted her any further than he could have thrown her, and given his present surroundings, that didn't amount to much.

Her grey-green eyes were never still, darting here, there and everywhere; so much so, he wondered if the moments when they appeared to be out of synch with each other were simply a reflection of his own inability to keep up with the constant changes.

And yet...and yet...perhaps it was the overall whiteness, but she had that indefinable quality some women are born with; a kind of wide-eyed 'please help me' innocence that many men find hard to ignore, despite all the risks they know they are running.

Planting a warm kiss on both cheeks, she curled up on the banquette next to his chair, coming to rest in a cloud of lime, citron, grapefruit, and mandarin; a perfume that was immediately recognisable since Doucette had only that morning listed the ingredients to him.

The last named was particularly apposite, since additional confirmation of her identity came with the brief glimpse he'd had of a canal boat tattooed on what Monsieur Leclercq quaintly called her right *mandarine*. Although firmly anchored, it was rising and falling in a tantalising manner as though riding an incoming tide.

'*Eau d'Hadrien*,' he said. There was no harm in snatching a few bonus points while he could.

Looking suitably impressed, his guest nevertheless managed to recover her composure in remarkably quick time.

'Monsieur Aristide Pamplemousse,' she countered. 'Late of the Paris *Sûreté*.' She savoured the words as though they referred to one of the chef's specials. 'No wonder Véronique refused to say who I was meeting.'

'You are not in your working clothes,' said Monsieur Pamplemousse. 'Don't tell me you have been defrocked.'

'It wouldn't be the first time,' said Maria. 'Anyway, I have had a career change. The habit went with my previous job.'

He tried to place her accent and, having failed, decided to stick with French.

'It must have been very sudden...'

'You could say that. Some offers happen faster than others. You turn a corner, and hey presto...'

'But before that,' he persisted, 'you had no qualms about dressing up as a nun?'

'Why should I? Don't tell me it is against the law.'

'I was thinking of the laws of propriety,' said Monsieur Pamplemousse. 'Some people might take exception to it.'

'You'd be surprised,' said Maria. 'Different people have different tastes. A lot of men go for that kind of thing.'

'Am I right in thinking it was you who chose this particular venue?'

'I happen to like old things,' said Maria. 'Not that I don't like new experiences too,' she added.

Glancing round the room, she took in the faded decor. 'This must be as old as Methuselah. Just look at that mirror. You can hardly see your face in it for all the scratches. As for the paintings; very Garden of Eden, if you believe in that kind of thing. Like how the world began – Adam and Eve and all that stuff, don't you agree?'

'I don't picture an old man with a beard watching over us, if that's what you mean,' said Monsieur Pamplemousse, 'or even an old lady with a beard, if it comes to that.

'It may be part of my early training but, like Lord Byron, I deny nothing, although I doubt everything. In the meantime I keep the Big Bang theory in reserve.'

Moistening her lips, Maria eyed him with new interest.

'Do you, now?'

'Although, even then,' he said hastily, 'I would have

trouble picturing there being nothing before the world came about...'

'You mean no foreplay...that kind of thing?'

Sensing he might be getting into rather deeper water than he had intended, Monsieur Pamplemousse reached for the bell push. 'I think it is time we ordered.'

The Assistant *Maître d'* must have been hovering outside, for he entered almost at once, notepad and a second menu at the ready.

'You choose,' said Maria. 'You're the expert.'

Ordering two glasses of champagne as an aperitif, Monsieur Pamplemousse stuck to his original plan; the egg and truffle concoction, risotto with scallops, and the soufflé Lapérouse, adding a bottle of Meursault to accompany the main course, and a steak *haché* with a bone on the side for Pommes Frites.

'I'm in your hands,' said Maria, when he looked at her enquiringly.

No sooner had the man departed than a commis waiter arrived with the champagne. It must be taken for granted in such surroundings.

He took heart in the fact that at least the risotto and the soufflé would take time to prepare. Otherwise, given the present rate of progress, he would be hard put discover all the things he felt it would be good to know, and there might not be a better opportunity.

With that end in view, he lingered over pronouncing on the wine when it was presented. Green-gold, it was full-bodied and...he couldn't help inwardly comparing it with his guest – full of promise.

'You do know the way to a girl's heart,' said Maria, when

they were alone at last. She sipped her champagne. 'What shall we talk about now?'

Monsieur Pamplemousse decided on the direct approach. He suddenly felt himself back in his old office at the Quai des Orfèvres, rather than a tiny room at Lapérouse.

'Who are you working for?'

Maria pulled a face. 'I was hoping it would be something nice.'

'*Vous êtes ravissante, mademoiselle,*' he responded. 'Is that what you would like to hear me say?'

She looked at him suspiciously. Then, somewhat to his surprise said: 'Only if you mean it.'

He was saved having to reply by the arrival of the first course.

'A girl's got her dreams,' said Maria, when they were alone again.

'Sometimes,' said Monsieur Pamplemousse, 'the reality can be less satisfactory than the dream. It is invariably more costly in the long run. I can only repeat the question. Who are you working for?'

'*Le Guide.* As if you didn't know.'

'I have been away,' said Monsieur Pamplemousse.

'But if you are not employed by them any more, why are you so interested in me?'

'How do you know I am not?'

If she was thrown, it didn't show. To her credit, she gave as good as she got.

'Word gets around. Come to that, who *are* you working for?'

Monsieur Pamplemousse ignored the question. 'You are not French,' he said.

'No,' said Maria. 'But so what?'

'Because, if you were French, you would know that we live by rules and regulations. It is all part of a Grand Design. French is not, as many outsiders believe it to be, simply the language of love; it is also the language of property rights, contracts and many other things to do with the law, and it is very exact.

'It began in 1804 with the Code Civil; Napoleon's monument to the French language, spelling out in 2,281 short edicts the rules governing everything in a person's life, from birth to death.

'Those rules have been added to over the years, eventually covering such mundane matters as the time it should take a concierge to clean each square metre of a courtyard, through the shape and constituents of a standard baguette, down to the size of a baby's bottle.

'With the passage of time, some have been discarded along the way in order to take account of the change in lifestyles. For example, once upon a time bars licensed to sell tobacco had to display a stylised red carrot outside their premises.'

Maria stared at him. 'People used to smoke carrots too?'

'No,' said Monsieur Pamplemousse patiently. 'It was because they always kept a fresh one inside their storage bins to stop the tobacco drying out.'

Maria snuggled up against him. 'I do love a man who knows about these things. But why are you telling me all this?'

'Because,' said Monsieur Pamplemousse, 'whatever it is you are up to, you won't get away with it. Many of the rules and regulations are openly ignored. However, when it comes to the crunch, if the authorities want to get you, they will. It may be something relatively small – like dressing up as a nun – but get you they will. There is no escape.'

'Ladies first,' said Maria. 'You still haven't answered my question. If you are no longer working for *Le Guide*, who *are* you working for?'

'Let us just say that for the time being I am acting on behalf of Monsieur Leclercq. It is a personal matter.'

'Ah, Monsieur Leclercq!' said Maria dreamily. 'He has only to look at me and my inside turns to water...' She put down her knife and fork, edged closer, and placed a hand on his knee. 'Some men have that effect on me.'

Ever alive to passing nuances, Pommes Frites looked up from his minced steak, assumed his 'here we go again' expression, and gave vent to a deep sigh as he gnawed away at the bone.

'There, there,' called Maria. 'I shan't bite.'

'Let us hope he feels the same way about you,' said Monsieur Pamplemousse. 'He can be very protective of me when the spirit takes him and he may be sharpening his fangs.'

'He doesn't look very fierce,' said Maria.

'Don't let that fool you,' said Monsieur Pamplemousse. 'It is a question of territories. In his book, treading on other people's is always a dangerous occupation.'

'Meaning?'

'As I say, I am looking after Monsieur Leclercq's interests and from all I have seen and heard it seems to me that just lately you have been trespassing a great deal in matters that don't concern you.'

'But they do concern me,' simpered Maria. 'Henri needs looking after.'

'Henri? I wasn't aware that you and he were on first-name terms.'

'Well, now you know.' Maria looked him straight in the eye. 'It was love at first sight, and I would be very concerned if anything came between us. For instance, I don't know what I would do if his wife got to hear about it. I know he is terrified I might blurt it out one day and spoil everything, but I also know if things came to what you call the crunch, I wouldn't be able to help myself.'

'And you think she would believe you?'

'She would if she saw all the things Henri has been buying me,' said Maria. She held up her left hand. 'This, for instance, and all that goes with it. I have the receipts. A girl has to protect herself these days.'

Monsieur Pamplemousse gazed at the ring. The stone itself looked as though it wouldn't have been out of place on the business end of a knuckle-duster. It must have cost the Director an arm and a leg.

'It is very big,' he admitted, for want of anything better to say.

'Now do you understand what I mean?' said Maria triumphantly.

'Nothing changes,' said Monsieur Pamplemousse. He pointed to the mirror.

'You see all those scratches you complained about just now? They were made by girls who were, as you put it, protecting their interests. In this restaurant's heyday they used to scratch messages on the glass to make sure any diamonds given to them by their paramours were real.'

'You mean...like this?' Before he could stop her, Maria reached up, pressed the ring and its stone hard against the mirror, and drew a wide arc across its surface.

It was probably intended as a flamboyant, devil-may-care

gesture, but the effect was so unexpected it was safe to say no one in the room, least of all Maria, was in any way prepared for it.

Filmed on a high speed camera and played back in slow motion it might have been possible to analyse the exact sequence of events, but in real time it seemed as though everything happened at once.

The shrill sound of protesting glass gave way almost immediately to an even higher-pitched shriek from Maria; the combination of the two resulting in a veritable stream of harmonics.

Musically, a persistent bleeping noise provided a rhythmic beat, whilst a loud howl from Pommes Frites as the stone became detached from its mounting and broke into several pieces, the largest of which landed in his steak, produced a satisfactory coda.

As the sounds died away, the door burst open and a sea of faces appeared.

'It is nothing,' said Monsieur Pamplemousse. '*C'est normale.*'

Removing the key finder from his jacket pocket, he held it up for all to see. 'Something must have set it off. It happens from time to time.

'Much more serious is the fact that there is a foreign body in my dog's steak *haché.*'

'A foreign body!' Entering the room, the Assistant *Maître d'* drew himself up to his full height. '*Impossible!*'

Pommes Frites, having taken a closer look at his dinner, gave another howl; this time in support of his master.

'*Asseyez-vous,*' commanded Monsieur Pamplemousse. '*Immédiatement!*'

He bent down and removed the offending object from Pommes Frites' bowl.

Holding it aloft between thumb and forefinger, he indicated the reflected light from the chandelier.

'If that isn't glass,' he said, 'I don't know what is!'

For a brief moment there was the kind of silence you could have cut with a knife.

'Glass!' repeated the Assistant *Maître d'*.

'Glass!' echoed Maria. 'What do you mean, *glass*?'

'Glass,' said Monsieur Pamplemousse, 'is a transparent solid made from a fused mixture of oxides. It is useful in many ways, but being highly brittle it should never be confused with diamonds.'

Maria glared at him, grabbed her handbag, and made for the door. 'Excuse *me*,' she said. 'I need to make a call.'

'Small pieces of glass,' continued Monsieur Pamplemousse, turning to the *Maître d'*, 'are also highly indigestible and not to be recommended when mixed in with any kind of food.'

The *Maître d'* signalled to one of his underlings.

'The matter will be attended to,' he said, leaving no room for doubt that it would be. 'In the meantime, you have my sincere apologies. I assure you, monsieur, it will not happen again.'

Left to his own devices, Monsieur Pamplemousse took out his mobile and dialled a number.

Doucette must have been in the kitchen, for it took her a while to answer. In the meantime, he guessed Maria was probably giving the Director hell.

'Doucette, please do me a favour. As you know, I no longer have a watch, but could you give it a few minutes, then call me back?

'No, Couscous…everything is fine…

'There is nothing whatsoever to worry about…' He was suddenly reminded of Monsieur Leclercq's telephone conversation on the plane.

'I will explain when I see you,' he added.

'*Oui*…some of the left-over prawn dish will be fine…'

While he was talking, a hitherto unseen waiter carrying a bowl of freshly minced steak for Pommes Frites came and went. Hearing raised voices in the corridor outside, Monsieur Pamplemousse hastily cut the call and put the phone down on the floor beside his chair.

He barely had time to relax before Maria reappeared.

From the look on her face, he wondered if she was on drugs and had taken a quick fix. Her eyes didn't shown any sign of dilation. If anything, they looked more purposeful, so he dismissed the idea.

Given that she also appeared to have renewed her lip-gloss in no uncertain manner, he felt more than ever glad he'd made the call home.

'No luck?'

She gave a noncommittal grunt.

'Bastard!'

Holding the ring aloft as though it were some eyeless archaeological relic newly unearthed from an Egyptian tomb, she collapsed onto the banquette.

'They do say love conquers all.' Monsieur Pamplemousse tried to offer a crumb of comfort.

'Believe that,' said Maria bitterly, 'and you'll believe anything! Just wait until I see him. Cheapskate!'

She looked as though she was about to launch into a long tirade, when she spotted something on the carpet.

'There's another piece of my so-called precious gem! Mind your dog doesn't tread on it...'

Seeing Pommes Frites prick up his ears, Monsieur Pamplemousse joined her in making a dive for the spot.

From his vantage point on the other side of the table Pommes Frites half rose, then changed his mind. It was clearly a case of an immovable object about to meet up with an irresistible force. Had he been given to making bets he would have put his money on his master any day of the week. Weight for weight, the girl didn't stand a chance.

But then, being an animal of noble and upright disposition, the prospect of foul play raising its ugly head didn't for one moment enter his mind. It wasn't until he saw a silk-clad leg shoot out that he had second thoughts, but by then it was too late.

He winced inwardly as heads collided, and for a fraction of a second both parties hovered in mid-air before falling to the ground.

Ending up gasping for breath, the girl on top of him and with a ringing noise in his head, Monsieur Pamplemousse was mortified. All too late, he realised he had become a victim of one of the oldest tricks in the world.

For the second time that day he felt arms encircling him; the main difference this time being that the hands that went with them were hardly still for a moment. It was worse, far worse than being frisked at an airport during a major security alert.

Gradually coming to, he realised the ringing was coming from a telephone. Reaching out with a free hand, he groped around blindly for his mobile and, as he did so, made contact with... He froze...Monsieur Leclercq's disastrous experience on the plane still fresh in his mind, he found himself momentarily wondering if it was the Director's phone rather than his, and if that there were the case, was it still in place? If so...

Opening his eyes, he saw to his relief Pommes Frites standing alongside him, the mobile in his mouth.

'*Alors!*' Giving his ever-resourceful friend and mentor a welcome pat, he relieved him of the handset and pressed the receive button.

'Is everything all right, Aristide?' Doucette's voice came through loud and clear.

'You asked me to call you.'

Monsieur Pamplemousse felt the body on top of him stiffen.

'No, I didn't,' he hissed. 'You must be imagining things.'

'Imagining things! What do you mean?' Doucette sounded aggrieved.

'I think you must have been having one of your attacks, Couscous...' said Monsieur Pamplemousse.

'Attacks! What attacks?'

'The...ones...you...are...prone...to...' he tried to spell it out as clearly as possible, hoping the message would get through. 'Don't move, I will be with you as soon as possible...'

Pressing the off button, he struggled without success to push Maria to one side, and he was still trying when the phone rang again.

'You sound out of breath, Aristide,' said Doucette. 'Why are you breathing so heavily?'

'It is Pommes Frites, Doucette,' said Monsieur Pamplemousse. 'You know how he hates the heat and it is very warm in here. We are in one of the small rooms... listen...'

Retrieving his other hand, he cupped both of them over the mouthpiece and went into his dog on heat routine.

'It may be very popular at staff parties, Aristide,' said Doucette, 'particularly near the end of the evening when everyone has had too much to drink, but...'

'You should get yourself a headset and leave your hands free,' said Maria. 'Be a multi-tasker like me.'

'Who is that?' asked Doucette

'It is a girl at the next table...' said Monsieur Pamplemousse. 'She is a little the worse for drink, and...'

'But I thought you said you are in a small room...'

'One of the *smaller* rooms...' Monsieur Pamplemousse paused as he heard a knock at the door. 'Listen, Coucous,' he said desperately. 'I have to go. Don't ring me...I will ring you.

'I am afraid my guest has been taken ill,' he said lamely, as the *Maître d'* entered. 'In the circumstances...'

'Of course, monsieur...' There was a moment's hesitation, accompanied by a barely discernable raising of an eyebrow. 'Would monsieur prefer a helping hand, a doctor, or *l'addition?*'

'*L'addition, s'il vous plait,*' said Monsieur Pamplemousse. 'As quickly as possible.'

Heading back home, Monsieur Pamplemousse turned right onto the Pont du Carousel, narrowly missing a couple of pedestrians who were trying to beat the lights. He realised with a shock he was in auto-drive. He had no recollection whatsoever of the first few minutes of his journey and the drive along the fast moving race track known as the Quai des Grands-Augustins.

Who could have blamed him after all that had happened?

In the cold light of day, a judge for one.

With that in mind, he slowed down rather than accelerating for the lights on the far side of the river in case they changed to red. A driver behind him, taken by surprise, leant on his horn.

There was a brief exchange of mimed unpleasantries as the man overtook him. There being no justice in this world, he made the lights before they changed, Monsieur Pamplemousse didn't.

To say Maria was a fast worker would have been the understatement of all times.

It was little wonder Véronique and Madame Grante were worried. How Monsieur Leclercq could possibly have given her a job – and as an adviser, no less – was beyond him.

In the conversational stakes she was probably more than a match for his boss.

He could picture it all: against a girl who doubtless did most of her thinking on her back rather than on her feet – a *grande horizontale* in the making if ever he'd seen one – Monsieur Leclercq wouldn't have stood a chance, but even so…

Going over the evening's events, he wondered if he was right to have thrown in the towel like he did, but clearly Maria had been of like mind. Following the last debacle with Doucette's phone call, she couldn't wait for it to be over.

One thing was certain. Something must be done about the matter, and quickly.

Taking a right turn in the Avenue de l'Opera, he spotted a gap in the line of parked cars and pulled in. It was time he phoned Jacques again and put him straight.

He got through almost immediately. From the background

noise it sounded as though he was on the Metro.

'It's a girl!'

'Congratulations! How much did it weigh?'

Monsieur Pamplemousse held the receiver away from his head. He was in no mood for jokes, especially ones in poor taste.

'The one going by the name of Péage. As it happens, I can let you have her picture.'

'Now you're talking.' Jacques did his best to sound contrite.

'I will do a printout and drop it in for you first thing tomorrow.'

'*Ciao. Dormez-bien.*'

'You must be joking,' said Monsieur Pamplemousse.

Feeling in a slightly better mood, he made the rest of the journey home in record time, and having put his car to bed for the night, took Pommes Frites for a quick walk around the block.

As he stepped out of the elevator on the fourth floor he felt for his keys.

'*Merde!*'

What with one thing and another, he must have left them in the restaurant. Unless it was the proverbial third thing, there shouldn't be any problem getting them back. For the time being, though, it was the final ignominy, having to phone Doucette again in order to be let into his own apartment.

'You told me on no account to answer the door,' said Doucette, when she opened it.

'I didn't bargain on losing my keys, Couscous,' said Monsieur Pamplemousse.

'What *has* been going on, Aristide? I couldn't make head nor tail of it over the phone. First you told me one thing, then another.'

'It was,' said Monsieur Pamplemousse, 'a constantly changing scenario. The problem is much bigger than I thought. And more complicated. I was dining with Monsieur Leclercq's new adviser.'

Switching his camera to 'playback', he showed Doucette the picture on the screen.

'Oh, dear,' she said. 'I do see what you mean.'

'She has to be working for someone else,' said Monsieur Pamplemousse. 'But for the time being, for whatever reason, she seems to have the Director wrapped round her little finger. Just as she had herself wrapped round me earlier on.'

'How very embarrassing,' said Doucette.

'I think,' said Monsieur Pamplemousse, 'that over the years they have probably seen most things at Lapérouse. Nothing surprises them any more.'

Over the warmed-up remains of the prawn dish he gave Doucette an edited version of the evening's events.

'You are always saying Monsieur Leclercq shouldn't be allowed out by himself,' said Doucette when he was through. 'It sounds to me as though he isn't the only one.'

'That was different,' said Monsieur Pamplemousse gruffly.

'Talking of the Director,' said Doucette, 'He phoned while you were out. He was speaking from home and it sounded urgent. He said, could you ring him back?'

'Aristide…' the Director's voice sounded muffled, as though he had his hand over the mouthpiece. 'We are in an *Estragon* situation.'

It didn't sound a promising opening. He decided to swallow his pride.

'Perhaps, monsieur, we should meet…'

'*Oui*. I think so too. Somewhere not too close to the office... Have you any suggestions?'

'How about the Luxembourg Gardens?' said Monsieur Pamplemousse. 'There is an entrance opposite rue Vavin where it joins rue d'Assas and rue Guynemer. Turn right when you are inside and follow the path round. I will be waiting just beyond the statue.'

Monsieur Leclercq sounded dubious. 'As I recall, Pamplemousse, the Jardin de Luxembourg is full of statues. You can hardly move for them. It is hard to tell one from another.'

'This one is of Sainte-Beuve,' said Monsieur Pamplemousse patiently. 'It is by a large Braille map erected for the benefit of the blind. You cannot possibly miss it. That part of the gardens is given over to the growing of fruit trees. It should be quiet at this time of the year.

'Assuming you will be coming by car, will find there is street parking in rue Guynemer itself. It is for a maximum of two hours, but that should give us ample time. You will need a card, but you can buy one at any *tabac*.'

'Aristide, as always, I admire your attention to detail,' said Monsieur Leclercq.

'Shall we say ten-thirty, monsieur?'

'Ten-thirty,' echoed the Director meekly.

'I hate to say it, Couscous,' said Monsieur Pamplemousse, as he began getting undressed later that evening, 'but I have been thinking...'

'...it is time I went to stay with my sister, Agathe.' Doucette finished the sentence for him.

'It would relieve me of one worry. I suspect that from now on I shall be in need of Pommes Frites' services day and night, and given that he can't be in two places at once...'

'There are times,' said Doucette, 'when I feel positively clairvoyant.' She pointed to a suitcase behind the door. 'What do you think I've been doing this evening? You can have my keys while I am away.'

'I hope it won't be for long,' said Monsieur Pamplemousse. 'And if I'm not there,' he added by way of consolation, 'at least you won't have to put up with her *tripes á la mode de Caen*.'

CHAPTER EIGHT

As things turned out, Monsieur Pamplemousse was glad he had opted for the least-populated part of the Luxembourg Gardens. Chairs were in short supply.

The mass of berries he'd seen on a yew tree suggested a hard winter ahead, but for the time being at least there was a sudden change in the weather. The wind had dropped, the sun was shining, and from being only a few degrees above freezing, the temperature had risen to 24 Celsius; 'a wall to wall ceiling of blue' in the words of a radio forecaster, waxing lyrical. It could have been a spring morning, except there was nothing in bud.

And, as ever, Parisians were making the most of it.

From where he was sitting, distant flurries from the tennis courts floated through the air, steady thwacks mingling with the sporadic thud of steel boules striking the wooden safety boards surrounding the Pétanque area. Above it all, there was the sound of tractors hurrying to and fro, taking advantage of the Indian summer to speed up the annual transfer of less hardy flora to their winter quarters. Bees in the nearby apiary must be scratching their heads.

And it was half term. That was something else he hadn't bargained on. The main part of the gardens was awash with small figures. Interspersed with an occasional series of shrill blasts from a police whistle, they more than added their mite to the overall buzz of activity.

Once again, he found himself instinctively glancing at his wrist only to draw a blank.

When things were back to normal he would do something about it. In the meantime...

...it wasn't like the Director to be late, so he was probably having difficulty finding somewhere to park.

But no, talk of the devil! The thought was still-born as a familiar figure, carrier bag in one hand, briefcase in the other, rounded a corner and headed in his direction.

As he drew near, the Director's face registered disappointment. 'No Pommes Frites, Aristide?' he exclaimed. 'How very unfortunate. I have been all the way to a dog *biscuiterie* in the 15th *arrondissement*.'

He made it sound like a trek to the North Pole, and Monsieur Pamplemousse was on the point of asking what the weather was like in those parts, when he was beaten to the draw.

'It is called Mon Bon Chien,' continued Monsieur Leclercq, 'An American lady runs it, and being something of a gourmet herself, she tells me her products not only contain no sugar or salt, but they are guaranteed free of all preservatives. Had I known about it earlier, for a small sum Pommes Frites could have had his name imprinted on the biscuits.'

'We have always brought him up not to read while he is at table,' said Monsieur Pamplemousse gravely.

His words fell on deaf ears.

'Quite right,' said Monsieur Leclercq. 'Old-fashioned values are worth preserving. All the same, I shall be interested to know what he makes of them. It could make an interesting entry for *Le Guide*.'

Clearly, the Director was in a more conciliatory mood than when they had last met, but if the biscuits were meant to be a peace offering, Monsieur Pamplemousse made sure it fell on stony ground.

'I will give them to him later,' he said coldly. 'For the time being he is in my car. Dogs are not allowed to enter the gardens by this gate. They are obliged to use the Gay Lussac entrance, or failing that, Royal Collard or the one at Observatoire Est on the opposite side of the gardens. Even then they have to be on a leash.'

'I trust you have left his window ajar?' said the Director. 'These sudden spells of hot weather can be very deceptive.'

'The windows on my 2CV are almost permanently ajar,' said Monsieur Pamplemousse. 'However, Citroën have more than made up for such lapses. The ability to park where others have failed is just one of the many reasons why I remain wedded to it.'

'Where there's a will, Pamplemousse, there is a way.' Monsieur Leclercq countered the intended thrust with a dismissive wave of his hand. 'I managed to squeeze my CX25 into the last two remaining places in the rue Guynemer. In fact, it was just outside the entrance gates you suggested.'

Monsieur Pamplemousse couldn't help wondering if the Director had paid for a second parking space. He wouldn't fancy his chances otherwise. On a day like today the ladies from the *Agents de Surveillance* would be out in force, ticket machines at the ready.

'The rear half was on a pedestrian crossing,' said Monsieur Leclercq in response to his question. 'I had a quiet word with the meter maid,' he added grandly. 'A pretty little thing. She said she hadn't seen my car, but I was to make sure it wasn't there the next time she went past in case she did. She kept me talking, which is why I am a little late.

'You will have read my note, of course,' he continued, seating himself in an adjoining chair. 'I would hate you to think I was in earnest about declaring Pommes Frites redundant. I had expected you to be in touch earlier, but...'

Monsieur Pamplemousse stared at him. In the heat of the moment he had completely forgotten the scrap of paper in his right jacket pocket.

'I have been carrying it around ever since you gave it to me,' he said, begging the question as he felt in his pocket. Holding it aloft, carefully making sure the back faced the Director, he read the message scrawled on the front.

'*Les mureilles ont des oreilles!*'

'Walls have ears!' It took a moment or two for the words to sink in. Then, suddenly, everything...the going out onto the balcony that first morning...the whispered exchanges...the unceremonious dismissal of Pommes Frites; all took on a new meaning.

It felt as though a great weight had been lifted from his mind. Thank goodness he hadn't screwed the paper up and thrown it away unread. He had been sorely tempted to do so at the time.

'In the circumstances,' said the Director, 'I considered it a necessary ploy. Given all the things that have been happening of late, I had almost come to believe the old adage, and that walls really do have ears. And yet, a sweep of the office by our security advisers has revealed nothing untoward.

'I have to admire the way you cottoned on to my meaning as quickly as you did. Your explosion of righteous indignation was masterly. As for your spur-of-the-moment resignation; it struck exactly the right note. Pommes Frites played along too. His howl was quite bloodcurdling.'

Congratulations dispensed with, Monsieur Leclercq sat back and took in the tranquil scene.

'You have chosen well, Aristide,' he said. 'It is a long time since I last visited these gardens and one tends to forget its many pleasures. There is something for everyone. I am, of course, familiar with the great avenues of chestnut trees and the flower-beds – Paris sets great store by its greenery – but I have to admit I was completely unaware of all these espaliered fruit trees laid out before me, like rows of giant candelabra. I must pay another visit when they are in leaf.'

'There are over six hundred varieties of apples and pears,' said Monsieur Pamplemousse. 'All of them labelled and dated. For that, we have to thank some Carthusian monks.'

'What a wonderfully satisfying task tending them must be for their successors,' said the Director.

'The simplest-looking tasks often conceal a great deal of hard work,' said Monsieur Pamplemousse. 'That is part of their strength. Think of all the pruning they require; the feeding and the patient training of the branches – those known as the *Palmette Verriers* have nineteen. Then there is the continual replacement of stock. Some of the trees are over a hundred years old. During the summer months, each and every fruit is enclosed in a paper bag before the wasps and the birds can get at them. For many of the staff it is a lifetime's work.'

'At least they have time to think,' said Monsieur Leclercq. 'Thinking time is very precious, Aristide. It is difficult to find peace and quiet in this day and age.'

He gazed benevolently at a loaded trailer as it went past. 'It is another world. I hardly know the name of some of the flora I see around me.'

'That was a pomegranate tree,' said Monsieur Pamplemousse. 'Its flowers are used in the manufacture of red ink.'

'Where *do* you learn these things, Aristide?'

'I am a snapper-up of unconsidered trifles, monsieur. It used to be part of my job.

Talking of which…' He decided to take the plunge.

'Yesterday evening,' he said, 'I dined at Lapérouse.'

The Director perked up. 'Did you, now? How was it? Glandier gave it a good report recently. I trust you partook of rather more than unconsidered trifles while you were there.'

'I think they deserve a special mention for the way they responded to an extremely difficult situation,' said Monsieur Pamplemousse. 'The staff could not be faulted. As for the meal…I would say the first course lived up to its promise, and the Meursault was excellent. Unfortunately, I didn't get as far as the main course…'

'It sounds as though you harbour doubts, Aristide.'

'It wasn't the food that gave rise to them,' said Monsieur Pamplemousse, 'it was the company…'

'Throughout its long history,' said Monsieur Leclercq, 'no one has ever visited Lapérouse solely for the food. In its early days it was chicken farmers conducting their business, during the third republic the *salons particuliers* were especially popular with those indulging in clandestine affairs – or worse. Prostitution was rife, *horizontales* were made welcome, and the laws at the time were such that they couldn't be prosecuted. Nowadays, people go there to savour its past glories.'

'I was in a *salon particulier* last night,' said Monsieur Pamplemousse. 'The Otéro.'

'Were you now?' Monsieur Leclercq didn't go so far as to say 'you gay dog!', but it was clear he thought it.

'It was not my choice,' said Monsieur Pamplemousse. 'Fortunately, thanks to Véronique, I had Pommes Frites with me.'

Reaching into an inner pocket, he produced a second copy of the photograph he had left at the Quai des Orfèvres for Jacques. 'This is a picture of my guest.'

To give him his due, Monsieur Leclercq didn't bat an eyelid. It was almost as though he had sensed what was coming.

'What did you think of her, Aristide?' he asked after a moment's pause.

'As you rightly say, monsieur, she is a pretty little thing, but...'

'She is not *comme il faut*?' Monsieur Leclercq finished the sentence for him.

Monsieur Pamplemousse gave a shrug. 'As the American singer, Dolly Parton, once said of herself: "It costs a lot of money to look this cheap."'

'I can vouch for that,' said the Director with feeling.

'I also suspect she probably changes with the wind.'

'Meaning?'

'One can hardly dislike her. But basically, Maria has the

attributes of a Japanese Geisha girl; she is all things to all people. Last night she merged in with the decor as to the manner born. As a travelling companion in the *première* compartment of a jumbo jet I can well imagine time would fly too...'

'Don't remind me, Pamplemousse,' groaned Monsieur Leclercq.

'These things happen,' said Monsieur Pamplemousse sympathetically. 'Now that I have met the girl, I think I understand more than I did when you first told me about her.

'As for the rest of the evening, it had its difficult moments; *par exemple*, when she used the mirror to test a ring someone had bought her and the stone shattered.'

'It did?' Monsieur Leclercq went pale at the thought. 'Was she very upset.'

'Had I been the person who gave it to her,' said Monsieur Pamplemousse, 'and had I been there when it happened, I would not have fancied being in his shoes.'

'It was a spur-of-the-moment decision on my part,' said the Director. 'I happen to know the owner of the shop. He is a person of the utmost discretion, so I was able to come to a private arrangement. He has special items he keeps for window display purposes only.'

'I somehow doubt,' said Monsieur Pamplemousse, 'if that would have gone down well with Maria.'

He was struck by a sudden thought. 'You didn't receive a call from her yesterday evening?'

'Certainly not,' said the Director. 'The only incoming call was yours.'

They sat in silence for a moment or two. The Director's mind clearly on other matters; Monsieur Pamplemousse

wondering who Maria had been talking to if it wasn't
Monsieur Leclercq.

'With great respect,' he said, when he judged the time was
right, 'given all that had gone before, how could you possibly
have given her the job?'

'I didn't exactly give it to her, Aristide,' said Monsieur
Leclercq. 'She made it perfectly clear it was that or else.'

'But...'

'But nothing, Pamplemousse!' The Director opened his
briefcase. 'As for what happened on board the plane...At the
time, given the way the flash kept going off, I thought she was
being particularly maladroit. It wasn't until I saw these...'
Rummaging through one of the inside pockets, he produced a
handful of glossy prints, and after first looking over his
shoulder to make sure no one else was around, handed them
across.

'Shortly after my return, these arrived through the post,
along with a brief note spelling out what she had in mind.'

A feeling of *déjà vu* came over Monsieur Pamplemousse as
he skimmed through the bunch. They were worse than he had
expected; far worse.

They reminded him of the time when the Director had been
photographed in a compromising situation involving a
washing machine in its spinning-drying mode. In practical
terms, they were nothing like it of course, but parallels could
be drawn. For someone whose watchword was anonymity,
the Director was remarkably accident prone. A walking target
might be a better description.

Lingering over the third print, a fully frontal self-portrait of
Maria, he cast a critical eye over it.

'It really is extraordinary the progress that has been made

with the camera side of mobile phones,' he said. 'The improvement in definition from even a year ago is truly amazing. Take this one of your *petite amie*. You can see every detail of her anatomy as plain as a pikestaff.'

Monsieur Leclercq gave a shudder. 'Given the choice, Pamplemousse, I would far rather look at a pikestaff! Secondly, let me make it clear once and for all, Maria is not my *petite amie*, she is *une petite coquine*! Mobiles are an invention of the devil. There should be a law against them.'

'I daresay if Eve had been granted the benefit of one in the Garden of Eden,' mused Monsieur Pamplemousse, holding up a two-shot, 'the world might have been a different place. Although I doubt it. If one is to believe the teachings of the Bible, she would have had no one else to call had she felt in need of being rescued, which I very much doubt would have crossed her mind anyway, but at least she had her fig leaves to fall back on.'

The Director looked over his shoulder. 'Careful, Pamplemousse,' he said nervously. 'Someone might creep up on us from behind.'

'If they do, we will most likely be arrested,' said Monsieur Pamplemousse. 'The Park police are extremely vigilant. Little escapes their notice. The blowing of whistles is one of their favourite occupations'

'In that case,' said the Director, 'we should be doubly careful. If they see us exchanging photographs we could be accused of peddling porn.

'Put yourself in my position, Aristide. I was desperate. I thought it better to keep her in my sights rather than have her roaming about like a loose cannon. I told myself that we live in troubled times and that perhaps the problem would go away.

'What is the Catholic Church coming to, Aristide?' he asked, putting the photographs back into his case. 'I know we live in a so-called secular society, but...'

'I don't think the Church enters into it,' said Monsieur Pamplemousse.

'You don't mean...' Monsieur Leclercq gazed at him. 'Are you suggesting I may not have been Maria's first *beau*? What do you think, Aristide? I respect your judgement in these matters.'

Privately, Monsieur Pamplemousse thought the Director most probably wasn't even Maria's fifty-first, but he decided not to labour the point.

'You are right about the photographs,' he said. 'I think she knew exactly what she was doing. I suspect the whole thing must have been part of a plan. As for phoning your wife, it had nothing to do with her memory; she had only to press the appropriate key to recall the last number you had dialled yourself.

'If you really want my opinion,' he said, 'I suggest Maria is no more of a nun than I am. She is, as my old mother would have said, "No better than she should be".'

'I always thought such girls were supposed to wear a number,' said the Director.

'That was in Maupassant's time,' said Monsieur Pamplemousse. 'The practice died out over one hundred and fifty years ago. Had she been wearing a number today it would be like the ducks consumed at the Tour d'Argent – well into the millions.'

'Ah, I knew I had read it somewhere,' said Monsieur

Leclercq vaguely.

'By all accounts,' continued Monsieur Pamplemousse, 'Maupassant was something of a sexual athlete and took little account of such mundane matters. It is little wonder he died of syphilis.'

Monsieur Leclercq went a paler shade of white. 'Do you think I ought to see matron, Aristide?'

'Only you can answer that question, monsieur.'

'What am I to do, Aristide?' asked Monsieur Leclercq, hastily changing the subject.

'Even now, I cannot bring myself to think of Maria as a wholly bad egg. She may be a trifle over-sexed, but that is simply the way she is. As you well know, Pamplemousse, some people are like that. They cannot help themselves. They are born that way.

'If she has a fault, it is that she is always borrowing my mobile, but since she has been with me she has made some very sound suggestions.

'It was she who suggested we tighten our security. Rambaud is a good man, but hardly on the cutting edge of what is required in today's world of high security. He has much in common with those superannuated usherettes one comes across in New York theatres who seem to go on and on, long past their "sell by" date. We live in troubled times and it wouldn't take much to overpower him. That being so, I have put him on paid leave for the time being.'

'And the present incumbent?'

'Bourdel? He came with the highest recommendation. Maria saw to that. I venture to think BRINKS wouldn't have employed him otherwise.

'To take an expression that I believe is in common usage by

members of your erstwhile occupation, Maria must be nobbled before it is too late.'

'Are you suggesting I should lean on her, monsieur?'

'I have no idea what the technical term is, Aristide,' said the Director, 'but if it means what I think it means, then by all means, go ahead.'

'From all I have seen and heard of her,' said Monsieur Pamplemousse, casting his mind over the previous evening's happenings, 'leaning on her is the last thing I would wish to do.'

'In that case, can you not find someone who will? You must still have contacts from the old days. People who are versed in such matters. It needs a person of discretion.'

'The two qualities don't always go hand in hand, I am afraid,' said Monsieur Pamplemousse. He tried floating an idea in the air. With luck, it might kill two birds with one stone.

'If you have something of that nature in mind, monsieur, could you not make use of your wife's Uncle Caputo in Italy? The one with the Mafia connections? He owes me one, as the saying has it. If you remember, I rescued his daughter when she was in Paris.'

'I think not,' said the Director. 'The only connection Chantal's uncle has with the catering business is that of extracting protection money from innocent *restaurateurs* who have nothing to fear in the first place. He derives a great deal of his income from such activities. He thinks nothing of going into a restaurant and, after admiring the china, saying wouldn't it be a pity if it all got smashed, suggesting they should take out some kind of insurance policy. The last time I mentioned a restaurant to him, thinking he might enjoy the food, all he said was: "You want it torched? Just say the word."

'I live in constant fear that his name might one day be connected to *Le Guide*. Sales in Italy would plummet.'

Monsieur Pamplemousse had a momentary vision of there being a symbol in *Le Guide* saying in effect: 'Torched by Uncle Caputo', but he kept it to himself.

'Having said that,' continued the Director, 'there is no reading his mind. For all his brash ways there is a thoughtful side to him. Only the other day he rang me to ask what size shoes I wear. I told him I have no idea. I leave such matters to my *chausseur.*'

'I think that was the best possible answer, monsieur.'

'Answers should fit the case, Aristide' said the Director. 'In the case we are discussing now there is only one possible answer. I need both you and Pommes Frites, and I need you as I have never needed anyone before. Now that you are, so to speak, officially *persona non grata* in your role as an inspector, I am in a position to offer you your old job back.'

'My *old* job, monsieur?'

'Head of Security for *Le Guide*. No one need suspect. You will be able to work undercover. I hardly need tell you how much depends on your success.'

'If I were to stay,' said Monsieur Pamplemousse, 'and despite everything, will Pommes Frites be reinstated?'

'If you are successful, Pamplemousse,' said Monsieur Leclercq. 'There is absolutely no question on that score.

'With that in mind, and to guard against all eventualities, I have sought legal advice. My understanding is that the ultimate fall-back position would be to have unassailable evidence regarding his culinary qualifications and judgement.

'The precedent in law is a *cochon d'Inde*, which was used by a well-known frozen food company to inspect vegetables shipped in from oversees. Apparently a guinea pig's instinct for sniffing out those that have been tainted with insecticides or some other substance is second to none. Almost one hundred per cent perfect.'

'Almost, monsieur?'

'Someone infiltrated some explosive material into a consignment of baby sweetcorn grown in Cambodia. One nibble and that was that. We wouldn't want a similar thing to happen to Pommes Frites.'

'I think I can safely safe say that it won't,' said Monsieur Pamplemousse. 'As you know, he was sniffer dog of his year when he was at Police College. Recognising explosives is one of his specialities.'

'A tasting has been arranged for tomorrow at *Le Guide*'s headquarters. I take it he won't object to being blindfolded? '

'Is that wise, monsieur?'

'Wisdom doesn't necessarily enter into legal arguments, Pamplemousse. More often than not, those who can afford the best lawyers win the day, and the simple answer in this case is that blindfolding all those taking part might be one of their requirements.'

Monsieur Leclercq looked at his watch and then made ready to leave.

'I had better not overstretch my meter maid's stock of good will,' he said.

Monsieur Pamplemousse watched as the Director's car accelerated away from its parking place on the pedestrian crossing just outside the entrance to the Luxembourg Gardens and turned right into rue Vavin before disappearing in the direction of *Le Guide*'s offices. No doubt he would be partaking of a Roullet Très Hors d'Age cognac before starting work. He certainly looked in need of one.

What was it the fat one in the old Laurel and Hardy films used to say when things reached a crisis point? 'Here's *another* fine mess you've gotten me into.' Or was it the thin one saying it to Olly? He must check with Glandier when he got the chance, otherwise it was the sort of trivial matter that could keep you awake half the night, and he had enough on his mind already.

He sighed inwardly as he opened the door to his own car a little further down the road.

It was all right for some. Why did he always say *oui* to these things?

Monsieur Pamplemousse's momentary irritation was echoed by the 2CV's suspension as Pommes Frites, blissfully unaware of his master's problems, clambered over the back of the passenger seat and made himself comfortable; a process that entailed several complete 360-degree turns before he was completely satisfied.

Having waited until he was comfortably settled, Monsieur Pamplemousse was about to set off when his phone rang.

'Your bird,' said Jacques, 'is English by birth. English mother and a Serbo-Croat father, and she's a *caravelle*.'

'*Comment?*'

'You've been out of the business for too long. You know...like an *entranneuse* specialises in working the bars, and a *michetonneuse* works café terraces, so a *caravelle* hangs around airports, waylaying lonely men, preferably high fliers first off the planes with their cabin bags on wheels. You can spot them a kilometre away.'

'You have been quick.'

'You gave me all that was needed,' said Jacques. 'As soon as I showed her picture to the vice squad it was a case of "say no more".'

'Is there a name for those who are airborne?' asked Monsieur Pamplemousse.

'Not yet,' said Jacques cheerfully. 'Just give it time.

'Anyway, it keeps them off the streets. Technically, it's now against the law for a girl to stand on a street corner wearing a low-cut blouse, but it'll take a lot more than that to put an end to the oldest profession in the world. Who's going to enforce it anyway? Jump to the wrong conclusion and you could end up in trouble.

'Maria perfected the art of picking on a likely-looking candidate and dropping something in their path – a handkerchief or a piece of paper, then turning her back as they drew near and bending down to pick it up. When her quarry rushed to her assistance and bent down too, their heads met, and...'

'Don't tell me,' said Monsieur Pamplemousse. 'I gather it is even more effective at 10,000 metres.'

'A young English-speaking French nun has a certain unique cachet with visitors from America; what they call arm candy for visiting tycoons. The phoney broken accent gets them every time. Maurice Chevalier in a skirt. If she scored less than one in twenty it was a bad day.'

'Does she have a record?'

'Not on paper. Let us just say she is "known about". The few people down the line who could have done something about her have probably benefited with a freebie or two, but she's never been brought in if that's what you mean.

'Lately, she seems to have gone quiet. I can try and find out more if you like...'

'I know *where* she is,' said Monsieur Pamplemousse. 'It's what she is up to and who she is really working for that bothers me. It would be good to have more background info.'

Without going into too many details, he gave Jacques a brief outline. It produced a satisfactory whistle at the other end of the line.

'It sounds to me like a case of history repeating itself,' said Jacques. 'It isn't the first time your boss has been photographed in what's known as a compromising situation. He does seem to make a habit of it.'

'And it probably won't be the last,' agreed Monsieur Pamplemousse. 'The world is increasingly divided into the takers of pictures and their subjects. Unfortunately, Monsieur Leclercq happens to be a natural-born subject, and every person who happens to own a digital camera automatically fancies himself or herself as a member of the paparazzi.'

'Give me the good old days and the *maisons des tolerance*,' said Jacques. 'At least you knew where you stood then. *And* it was considered much more respectable. Any knowledgeable visitor to Paris wanting a bit of extra mural excitement would ask a taxi driver to take them to 31 Boulevard Edgar Quinet. British Royals, turning up incognito, simply said: "Take me to the Sphinx."'

Jacques was onto his favourite subject.

'Did you know one of the main investors was a bank? In many ways the Sphinx was ahead of its time; a model employer. The rooms had air conditioning. The girls enjoyed three weeks' holiday on the Riviera every year. And they do say it had a wonderful wine list.'

'I wasn't around then,' said Monsieur Pamplemousse dryly. 'Neither was Maria.'

'*Touché!* But if you ask me, whoever is behind it all has your boss by what *les Anglais* aptly call "the short and curlies". I take it all this is strictly *entre-nous...*'

'Right in one.'

'I daresay we could have her picked up...'

'I think that could be a big mistake.'

'In that case, if you want to find out more about her background, why not get in touch with your English friend. What's his name? Pickering? It could be quicker in the long run. And safer, if you know what I mean. It'll save us finding reasons for doing it and the fewer people who know about it the better.'

Monsieur Pamplemousse considered the options for a moment. Jacques was right. It really was a classic case of what Mr Pickering would have called 'having someone by the short and curlies'. The French equivalent – *avoir quelqu'un à sa merci* – didn't have the same down-to-earth ring to it. He wouldn't dare say it to the Director's face, but as Pickering was fond of pointing out; French was the language of the ruling classes, whereas English was the language of the working classes.

'Anything else while I'm at it?' Jacques broke into his thoughts.

'Do you have any contacts at BRINKS, the security people?' asked Monsieur Pamplemousse.

'What do you need to know?'

'I am interested in one of their employees. A certain Bourdel...Paul Bourdel.'

'What's it worth?' Jacques' response was guarded.

'I'll let you choose the wine when we have that lunch,' said Monsieur Pamplemousse.

'*Ciao*,' said Jacques.

Mr Pickering was in a chatty mood when he answered the phone. Because of the slightly mysterious nature of his calling; a grey area to do with national security and therefore not up for discussion, he cropped up in Monsieur Pamplemousse's life from time to time, and over the years they had struck up a warm friendship. It took a lot to faze him.

'How's the weather?' he asked.

'Springlike,' said Monsieur Pamplemousse.

'It's raining cats and dogs here,' said Mr Pickering gloomily. 'Still, mustn't grumble. It's good for the garden.'

'Tell me, what did you have for breakfast this morning?'

'The usual, I'm afraid...' said Monsieur Pamplemousse. '*Croissant...brioche au sucre...*'

'Both still warm from the first baking of the day, I imagine...'

'Naturally...*Jus d'orange* – freshly squeezed. *Café*.'

'Ah, how I envy you. On the other hand, I shouldn't complain; there is a dreadfully depressing sameness about breakfasts all over the world. It's just that in England we lean towards cereals. There is a kind of holier-than-thou air about them; untouched by human hand from beginning to end, including my own, I have to admit. It is the packaging I object to most of all. Everyone looks so infernally cheerful. Then there is all the wording on the boxes saying how much good it will be doing you, although I have read somewhere there is as much nutritional value in the cardboard as there is in the contents.

'That apart, I can't stand the breakfast table being littered with them. It is a very bad start to the day. Mrs Pickering is thinking of knitting some covers. Anyway, how can I help you?'

'What do you know about prostitutes?' asked Monsieur Pamplemousse.

'As far as I am aware, there aren't many in our part of the world,' said Mr Pickering. 'Before we moved here, I'm told there used to be a certain amount of hanky-panky going on at weekends during the hot weather; occasional barbecue parties where the men threw their car keys into the swimming pool at the stroke of midnight. Then the ladies would dive in and fight for possession. That seems to have gone out of fashion.

'Nowadays the women just laugh and say "fetch them yourself". Not that we ever took part in that kind of thing, of course,' he added hastily. 'Mrs Pickering has breathing problems if she stays under water for too long.'

'I mean working prostitutes,' said Monsieur Pamplemousse. 'I am interested in one in particular. She was born in the UK.'

'Ah, that may take a little longer,' said Mr Pickering. 'When would you like to know?'

'Tomorrow will do,' said Monsieur Pamplemousse.

'Hold on a moment,' said Mr Pickering. 'I'll just turn the radio down.'

The call over, Monsieur Pamplemousse dialled another number. It was picked up almost at once. He was wrong about Martine Borel. Not only was she still at the same address, she recognised his voice instantly.

'Caller identification,' she said briefly, in response to his congratulations.

'I have a problem,' said Monsieur Pamplemousse, masking his disappointment. 'Or, perhaps I should say, *we* have a problem.'

'You mean…similar to the last one?'

'Not dissimilar. It would be good to see you. Soon, if that is at all as possible.'

There was a moment's pause followed by the sound of pages being turned.

'Today and tomorrow are not good, unless…how are your evenings?'

'In a word,' said Monsieur Pamplemousse, 'free.'

'In that case,' said Martine, 'you could join me in an experiment…*gigot de sept heures*. They say that after seven hours the lamb is tender enough to be eaten with a spoon. If we make it eight o'clock this evening it will have been cooking for ten.'

With memories of her *pot-au-feu* still fresh in his mind, it was an offer too good to refuse.

'Only if you will allow me to bring the wine,' he said. Les Caves Auge in the Boulevard Haussmann, Paris's oldest wine shop, was on his way home. A return visit was indicated.

'And Pommes Frites too, I hope,' said Martine.

'I shan't be able to look him in the face if I leave him behind,' said Monsieur Pamplemousse. 'He is already licking his lips.'

As he terminated the call, Monsieur Pamplemousse heard a tap on his windscreen, and looking up he saw a meter maid using the bonnet of his car as a writing desk.

It was a pity Monsieur Leclercq wasn't with him. It might have been a salutary reminder of the fact that not only was there no justice in the world, but even the prettiest of little things could have their downside.

On the other hand, the chances were that it would be like water off a duck's back. Some people never learnt.

CHAPTER NINE

Crossing the Seine via the Pont de Bir Hakeim for the second time in three days, Monsieur Pamplemousse couldn't help wondering if Madame Grante and Jo Jo were watching the passing scene from the window of Véronique's apartment further downstream.

In the Place de Costa Rica he turned left into the rue Raynouard and found a parking space almost exactly opposite the entrance to Maison de Balzac. Crossing the road, he looked down at the little blue-roofed house, with its green shutters and immaculately kept garden. Despite being stuck in a kind of time-warp and shrouded in darkness, the semicircular front porch still managed to looked welcoming and friendly, which was more than could be said of some of the entrances to the vast apartment blocks on either side, with their vast plate-glass doors and uniformed security guards.

Making his way up the hill towards Mademoiselle Borel's block, he came across a plaintive handwritten notice attached to a lamppost, pleading for news of a cat that had fallen from a seventh-floor window. Cats led charmed lives. Even so, he didn't fancy its chances. It must have used up most of its allotted number on the way down.

Presenting his credentials to a poker-faced man in the marble foyer, he led the way round a flower-filled rock garden towards a bank of four lifts, conscious as he did so that their every move would be recorded.

If the man remembered him from his last visit, he didn't let on. The same flowers were in bloom, confirming his initial suspicions that they were probably vacuumed every morning rather than watered. He wouldn't have dared touch one to find out. That, too, would be preserved on disc or tape.

Arriving on the tenth floor, he crossed the thickly carpeted vestibule, pressed a button on a door facing him, and while waiting recalled the first time he had visited Martine Borel.

That was when he discovered that not all computer boffins sported beards and wore steel-rimmed glasses. Instead, he had been momentarily knocked for six by the person who greeted him; cool, and smelling of what was then the 'in' perfume – Bigarade.

As the door opened he was relieved to find nothing, not even the perfume, had changed.

Pommes Frites bounded on ahead with a proprietorial air, made a half circuit of the room, stopped by a door leading to the kitchen for an appreciative sniff, then just as speedily returned to base, wagging his tail.

'I do apologise...' began Monsieur Pamplemousse.

'There is no need.' Martine Borel gave her four-legged visitor a welcoming hug. 'It is good to know everything meets with his approval...'

To Monsieur Pamplemousse's relief it was a case of taking up the threads as though they saw each other every day.

Martine ushered him towards a black leather armchair, one of a pair set near the picture window running almost the entire length of one wall.

A glass-topped table between the chairs had been set with two tall and recently chilled champagne glasses, one on either side of an ice bucket.

The arrangement of the furnishings was remarkably similar to Véronique's, as was the view across the Seine; in Passy, the Eiffel Tower was never far away.

Removing an already opened bottle from the ice bucket, Martine wiped the bottom of it dry with a napkin. While she was filling the glasses he took stock. Her make-up was, as ever, understatedly impeccable. A few grey hairs, perhaps, but the gold bangle on her wrist was the same, and the absence of rings suggested she was still Mademoiselle Borel.

It occurred to him how similar she and Vérnonique were. They even dressed alike, except Martine favoured green rather than brown, to match her emerald eyes. Perhaps these extra niceties also went with living in the 16th.

'You haven't changed,' he said.

'Neither have you...' She eyed him quizzically as she handed him one of the glasses. 'A few more grey hairs, perhaps.'

He raised the glass to his nose. The last time it had been a Californian white: Château Bouchamie Carneros, if his memory served him correctly; this time it was pink, refreshingly *pétillant*, and equally elusive.

'Think Bugey,' said Martine.

He placed it now: Cerdon, a sparkling wine made by the Champagne-method in the mountainous area to the west of the Savoie. She had caught him out again.

'Tell me the worst,' said Martine, after he had given her a rough outline of *Le Guide*'s problem. 'I take it you still have everything on a mainframe computer? As I remember it, a Poulanc DB23, 450 series. That is still in use?'

'It is,' said Monsieur Pamplemousse. 'But following the previous attack, we now have a new system in place. Preliminary work on the guide no longer takes place on the main computer. It has been divided into separate work-stations, one for each of the twenty-two regions of France.

'Theoretically, Monsieur Leclercq is the last person to see each entry via a printout, and he checks every detail with the proverbial fine-tooth comb before giving the OK for it to go through to the DB23, where it is assembled as a whole.'

'So it isn't exactly a repeat of the last time you were infiltrated?'

Monsieur Pamplemousse shook his head. 'On that occasion the hard disk on the DB23 was stolen and reprogrammed. This time it is more insidious and therefore potentially much more worrying. The first occasion would have been a disaster, a criminal act easily recognisable as such by the general public. Hence it would have been easier to recover from without leaving *Le Guide* with too much egg on its face.'

'Fragmentation has its advantages,' said Martine. 'Presumably the stations themselves are not connected to the outside world?'

'The hope was it would make the system impregnable.'

Martine looked sceptical. 'So what is happening this time?'

'It began with tiny changes being made to individual items by some person, or persons unknown, after they had been passed by the Director: essential pieces of information were being altered in such a way as to make it look like sheer carelessness, something calculated to undermine people's trust in *Le Guide*.

'*Par exemple*, early on we came across an entry saying Paul Bocuse is closed four days of the week.'

'That would have thrown the cat among the pigeons.'

'Indeed. Fortunately, we picked up on it, otherwise knives would have been out in Collonges-au-Mont-d'Or!'

'Is there a recognisable pattern to the changes?'

'In the beginning there was. Unfortunately, whoever is responsible seems to have grown more confident with time and the whole thing has begun to escalate.' Monsieur Pamplemousse cited the recent changes relating to the Tour d'Argent's entry.

'So it's panic stations?'

'The publication date in March may sound a long way away, but the reality is that unless something is done quickly we shall never make it, and that will be a black mark in itself.'

Martine replenished their glasses. 'Entering a computer is much like cracking a walnut. Once you are through the outer shell you can introduce a worm, which will feed on the inside fruit to its heart's content. The problem is how to get through the hard exterior in the first place.'

'Which is why I am here,' said Monsieur Pamplemousse.

'Tell some people a thing is impossible and they immediately see it as a challenge,' said Martine. 'That's what hackers are all about.

'Data security is big business. The craft of "intrusion protection" is an official job description – they are called "sniffers", and part of their work is trying to see how to break into systems. A good many start out as programmers. There is no better introduction.

'Only one thing is certain, there are people out there whose main aim in life is to keep ahead of the game. It is our function to try and beat them to the call.'

'*Excusez moi.*' Monsieur Pamplemousse made a face as his phone rang.

Signalling to Pommes Frites, Martine discreetly made her way towards the kitchen. Pommes Frites obeyed the call with alacrity, licking his lips as he followed on behind.

Activating his mobile, Monsieur Pamplemousse heard a familiar voice at the other end. 'You have been quick,' he said.

'Knowing which buttons to press helps,' said Mr Pickering. 'If you have one piece of information about a person you can almost always find more.

'In the case of your young lady, I struck gold almost at once by playing around with the name Péage, wondering what one would do to Anglicise it. Quite simply, the answer is – take away the "é".

'Her maiden name was Crescent...Deirdre Crescent, but for some unknown reason she was always known as Maria. According to the records, she is twenty-four, but looks much younger. Father was possibly a refugee from Eastern Europe who came to do the garden. In my day, when she was small she would have been known as "the school cert".'

'*Comment?*'

'It is an English joke to do with exams. Rather difficult to translate, I'm afraid. But take it from me, it was an augury of things to come.

'She was born in Totteridge and Whetstone. It sounds like a firm of estate agents, but in fact it's a station on our Northern Underground line. Rather out in the sticks. Such details are important in England; we place great store by them. They conjure up an immediate picture. Living in Harrow-on-the-Hill is one thing, but someone born in Totteridge and Whetstone might well kick over the traces sooner or later. In Maria's case it was sooner.

'She had what is known in the trade as a "loose eye", which she used to good effect when she was at school. It was a kind of party trick that also became a weapon of self-defence.

'When she was eighteen she married a Captain Page. Ex-British army, although there is no record of which regiment he was in. At the time he was dabbling in used cars in London's Warren Street; that and real estate.

'He also wasn't averse to passing his new bride around among his friends in the motor trade – for a small fee, of course. Afterwards he sold the photographs on. She stood it for six months, then ran away to Paris and hasn't been seen since.

'The last that was heard of her she was living on a canal boat somewhere in north-eastern France.'

'That is it?'

'I'm afraid so. At least as far as this side of the Channel is concerned. If I find out any more I will let you know. I hope I haven't interfered with your dinner.'

'On the contrary,' said Monsieur Pamplemousse. 'You have whetted my appetite.

You probably wouldn't believe me if I told you how long it has been cooking.'

'Now you have whetted mine,' said Mr Pickering. 'I will have a word with Mrs Pickering.'

Monsieur Pamplemousse offered up his thanks and promised to be in touch if he needed anything else.

He stared at the instrument in his hand. The information

wasn't exactly world shattering, but at least it confirmed all that Jacques had told him and helped build up a picture. Guilot had certainly been right about the name change. He had guessed Péage sounded more exotic to foreign ears. Living on a canal boat explained the tattoo as well.

He wondered if she would put in an appearance at tomorrow's tasting.

'I have been thinking.' Martine broke into his thoughts as she came back into the room.

'It seems to me there are three questions that need to be addressed.' She ticked them off on her fingers. 'Who? Why? and How? Not necessarily in order of importance. If you solve any one of those,' she continued, unwittingly echoing Mr Pickering's words, 'it will inevitably lead you to the others. I would suggest for a start it is most likely someone within your own organisation.

'I would also suggest you are holding in your hand a very likely means.'

Monsieur Pamplemousse stared at his mobile. 'This?'

'Not that particular one,' said Martine. 'It is, if I may so, somewhat out of date.'

'Sticks and stones...' began Monsieur Pamplemousse.

'...may break my bones,' said Martine, 'but never criticise a man's mobile. It is very emasculating.'

'I happen to like buttons that are easy to find in the dark,' said Monsieur Pamplemousse. 'I have enough trouble getting my fingers on the right ones as it is.'

'I only said that,' said Martine, 'because if you have someone in mind it would be good to know what model they are using.'

Monsieur Pamplemousse was reminded of the Director's words: *She is always using my mobile.*

'I think I can safely say it is the latest model.'

'Was,' corrected Martine. 'New ones appear almost as fast as we speak.'

'Tell me more,' said Monsieur Pamplemousse.

Martine looked at her watch. 'Why don't I do that over dinner? If we leave it any longer *gigot de sept heures* will become eleven-hour lamb, and as it is my first essay into the realms of molecular gastronomy, I would value your expert opinion.'

Having seated Monsieur Pamplemousse at an already laid table in the kitchen, she removed a large casserole dish from the oven, and while he was opening his bottle of wine – a Croze Hermitage Tête de Cuvée from Yann Chave – began serving it out.

'The lamb is milk fed from the Pyrénées. Two days ago I began by rubbing in salt and some thyme. This morning I pre-heated the oven to seventy degrees centigrade, wiped the leg clean of any excess salt, browned it in olive oil and placed it in the casserole – it needs a tight-fitting lid, like this one. After that I prepared all the other ingredients: carrots, onions; a *bouquet garni* of fresh thyme, rosemary, and a bay leaf of course; then I added garlic to the dish, and later still, some sliced potatoes...

'Earlier today I reduced around a third of a bottle of white wine until it was syrupy and passed that through a sieve to make a sauce in the roasting tray.'

While she was talking, Martine prepared a liberal helping in a bowl for Pommes Frites.

'It was lucky for both of us that you had time to answer the phone,' said Monsieur Pamplemousse.

'I know it sounds very labour intensive,' Martine placed

one of the plates in front of him while he poured the wine, 'but it isn't really. Besides, it almost becomes a labour of love. You keep wondering if all is well inside its cocoon.'

Monsieur Pamplemousse applied the side of his fork to the meat. It was like cutting through butter.

For a moment or two, apart from a lapping sound coming from a corner of the kitchen, they ate in silence.

'It is,' said Monsieur Pamplemousse at last, 'quite the most delicious lamb I have eaten for a long time. Congratulations!'

He tasted the wine. To his relief it didn't let him down. The underlining flavour of olives and thyme complemented the food; the slight acidity gave it freshness.

'Don't thank me,' said Martine. 'Thank my current cookery guru, Hervé This. He is the one who brought science into the French kitchen. The recipe itself comes from an English chef – Heston Blumenthal. It was from his Slow Food period. Nowadays he is also deeply into technology and the pursuit of excellence.'

'They are not alone,' said Monsieur Pamplemousse. 'It is all part of the process of evolution. Gastronomy has never really stood still since Carême turned cooking into an architectural art form. Escoffier followed on, raising its status still further. Nowadays we live in a restless age.

'Apart from Hervé This, we have Marc Veyrat, Robuchon, Ducasse, Gagnaire and many others. Spain has Ferran Adrià at El Bulli. America has Thomas Keller's French Laundry, Harold McKee, with his extraordinary books on the chemistry of food, and Jean-George Vongerichten in New York. I have also read that if you go into the kitchens of Grant Achatz's restaurant in Chicago you will look in vain for a stove as we know it. Fragrance is the order of the day, and it is all brought about in stainless-steel cylinders.

'People in all walks of life are forever searching for perfection. If it isn't a new taste sensation it is mobile telephones.'

'I can take a hint.' Martine looked suitably penitent.

Adding another slice of meat to Monsieur Pamplemousse's plate, she took a deep breath.

'Not to bore you on the subject, but historically, once upon a time bigger was best. Then a researcher at Bell Laboratories in America developed a tiny gear wheel that was so small – around the diameter of a human hair, they couldn't find a use for it, so for fun he turned it into a bracelet for an ant's leg. It didn't do much for the jewellery trade; come to that, it didn't do a lot for ants either, but in the fullness of time it spawned a whole new industry called nano-technology. Now, small is beautiful.

'Mobiles are not only getting smaller by the day, but at the same time they are becoming so crammed with gadgets they are starting to suffer from what is known as "feature creep". They are like Swiss Army knives. Fascinating to play with, but who needs to get stones out of horse's hooves these days?

'Now that it is possible to combine mobile technology with satellite-based navigation, people will be able to point their mobile at any hotel or restaurant and, at the press of a button, it will tell them everything they need to know.'

'Monsieur Leclercq won't be very happy,' said Monsieur Pamplemousse.

'It is something he will have to come to terms with,' said Martine. 'But at the same time, for many people part of the joy of travelling is in finding things out for themselves.

Planning ahead is part of the pleasure. They also value the opinion of someone they can trust.

'One shouldn't ignore other factors. Partly, it is a case of cause and effect. After 9/11 many Americans gave up flying and took to their cars because they felt safer. Result: deaths on the road rose by a measurable amount.

'Someone in France invents a new perfume smelling of teak, and trees in the rain forests of Brazil trees are chopped down to extract the essence.

'The really major down-side of mobile phones is the other uses they can be put to, such as triggering off things from a long distance.

'The bomb that killed over two hundred people in a Bali nightclub was detonated that way. Then came the bombing in Madrid; one hundred and ninety-one people on ten commuter trains killed during a three-minute period. After that came the London Under-ground bombings.'

'But could one be used to break into *Le Guide*'s files?'

'There is no reason why not. Current models are perfectly capable of scanning documents. Once scanned, the information can be compressed and tidied up electronically.

'The Xerox Research Centre in Grenoble has developed a phone that is capable of photographing anything up to ten pages at a time and turning it into black and white editable text ready for transmitting by fax or any other way you wish.'

Monsieur Pamplemousse gave a sigh. 'Where will it all end?'

'Things have a habit of going the full circle,' said Martine.

'Currently, mobiles are in much the same position as television receivers were a few years ago. Remember Bruce Springsteen's song, "57 Channels and Nothing On"? He ended up blasting his to pieces with a .44 Magnum. That was in 1992. Think how it would go now. More is not necessarily better.'

'I shall hate you for the rest of my life,' suggested Monsieur Pamplemousse, paraphrasing the song he'd seen advertised on a hoarding only a few evenings ago.

'Something like that.'

'And mobile telephones?'

'When things reach saturation point, people will turn to something else. The joy of taking out an old photographic album is already a thing of the past for many families; they have so many images stored on their computer. It could be due for a revival.'

'I can't wait,' said Monsieur Pamplemousse. 'So to sum up, someone could work on our files at their leisure and afterwards feed it back into the system?'

'If they are computer literate and in a position of being able to choose their moment. That is why I feel it is likely to be someone inside.'

Martine began clearing the table. 'Would Pommes Frites care for a little more?'

'Yes and no,' said Monsieur Pamplemousse. 'Yes, I am sure he would. No, he shouldn't. He has an important day ahead of him tomorrow and he needs all his faculties.'

Martime listened as he explained about the forthcoming tasting.

'Things *are* getting serious,' she said. 'In that case, he had better not have any of this.' She produced two bowls of a chocolate-coloured dessert from her refrigerator.

'I have added a little Calvados and it wouldn't be good news if he woke up tomorrow morning with a hangover.

'It is one of Monsieur This's inventions: Chocolate Chantilly. Molecular gastronomy at its best. If you know what happens to food when you cook it, you can make it work for you rather than against you. It may look and taste like cream, but I guarantee it is all in the mind.'

Monsieur Pamplemousse sampled his. Ambrosia was the only word to describe it. 'I daresay a small spoonful wouldn't come amiss,' he said, aware that his every movement was being watched.

From the expression on Pommes Frites' face a moment later, he was clearly of the same opinion.

'You are in the wrong business,' he said to Martine. 'If you ever think of opening a restaurant I guarantee you would have a Stock Pot in no time at all.'

Martine shook her head. 'Perish the thought. I value my freedom too much.'

'Returning to basics,' said Monsieur Pamplemousse. 'What if two people share a phone? Wouldn't the other person realise what was happening?'

'They could be using separate SIM cards,' said Martine, after a moment's thought.

'Does that mean…?'

'I think I know the answer to "who",' said Monsieur Pamplemousse simply. 'That's two down and only one to go.'

'In that case, what is the problem? I am not exactly looking for work, but if you want to take me on board and make it official…'

'It is very kind of you,' said Monsieur Pamplemousse, 'but we need to tread carefully. Sending out the wrong signals could be dangerous.'

He filled her in with the rest of the picture.

'I take your point,' said Martine. 'I understand the English have an apt phrase for it.'

'They call it the "short and curlies" syndrome,' agreed Monsieur Pamplemousse. 'You see the predicament.'

He looked around, aware that for some reason Pommes Frites, was on his feet, padding restlessly to and fro.

'Perhaps the Calvados wasn't such a good idea after all,' said Martine.

'It could be a call of nature,' said Monsieur Pamplemousse. 'But I think he is suffering from premonitions. I recognise the symptoms.

'Anyway.' He rose to his feet. 'It has been a lovely evening and it has helped clear my mind. I can't thank you enough.'

'All good things come to an end,' said Martine.

'One day of these days,' said Monsieur Pamplemousse, 'you must meet my wife. But first I would like to introduce you to her sister. She would benefit from a few lessons, especially when it comes to *tripes à la mode de Caen*.'

'I promise to read up on the subject,' said Martine. 'I'm sure Monsieur Blumenthal will have some ideas; like serving it alongside some deep-fried oranges in batter perhaps...'

'Anything would be an improvement,' said Monsieur Pamplemousse.

Bending down, Martine gave Pommes Frites a farewell pat. 'Good luck for tomorrow.'

'Sparing his blushes,' said Monsieur Pamplemousse, 'he has one unique quality that sets him apart from other dogs: discrimination. Given a choice, he doesn't automatically gobble down the first thing he comes to. He sniffs everything, and only then does he go for what in his opinion is the best.'

It was impossible to know if Pommes Frites had taken in what was said about him, but during the drive home he appeared lost in thought. Normally the most accommodating of passengers, anticipating corners and bends like a seasoned pillion passenger on a motorcycle, he had perfected the art of shifting his large frame at exactly the right moment. But when his mind was on other things, keeping a straight course demanded Monsieur Pamplemousse's undivided attention, so he wasn't sorry when the journey came to an end.

His answerphone showed there had been four calls while they were out; one from Jacques, two from Doucette, and the fourth from Sicily. He rang Doucette back first.

She sounded relieved. 'I was getting worried, Aristide.'

'I have been well looked after, Couscous. You will never guess what I was given to eat. *Gigot de sept heures.*'

'No wonder you are late back,' said Doucette. 'I hope you won't expect it too often in the future. Guess what we had...'

'Not...'

'I am afraid so.' Doucette lowered her voice. 'Agathe said she knew if she didn't cook it I would be disappointed.'

'The answer,' said Monsieur Pamplemousse, 'may lie in the molecules.'

'You must be joking,' said Doucette. 'Don't tell her that. She will have a fit.'

Monsieur Pamplemousse continued undeterred. 'I have put out feelers on the subject. In the meantime, keep smiling, Couscous. Worse things happen at sea.'

Jacques must have been awaiting his call. He answered halfway through the first ring.

'BRINKS were pretty cagey about your man. He is no more a member of staff than I am. They immediately went cold when I mentioned his name. Quoted the Data Protection Act, would you believe…'

'They were within their rights, of course,' said Monsieur Pamplemousse.

'Does that make it any better? Anyway, twisting their arm, I gleaned the fact that he was with them for a short while; long enough to pinch one of their uniforms.

'I didn't tell them I knew where it was. For what it's worth, they let fall the fact that he's an "ink addict". Not that that means much these days; tattoos are currently the "in" thing. And they aren't all stick-ons either; applying the needle is a big money-spinner. If the customers are female, they often want them done in the most surprising places, and that costs…'

'Or so I'm told,' Jacques added hastily.

'I believe you,' said Monsieur Pamplemousse. 'Thousands wouldn't.'

'Silly question,' said Jacques, 'but do you have a photo?'

'It wouldn't do you much good,' said Monsieur Pamplemousse, thinking of the dark glasses.

'I could have a go…' he began, and then broke off as a series of distant bells began ringing in his head; the phoney accent, Maria's tattoo…'I think I know where I might be able to get hold of one. Leave it with me.

'Also, just to warn you, it could be another case of my giving you the wrong name. You might try under Dubois…'

'Dubois? Dubois…wasn't he the *vilain* who cropped up the last time you had a computer break-in? Had it in for your boss; something to do with an old score he wanted to settle.'

'Old isn't the word,' said Monsieur Pamplemousse. 'It goes back to the early Sixties when Monsieur Leclercq was an inspector. The last big amendment to the Code Napoleon had just come into force – the *Code de la Consommation* – and he caught Dubois trying pass off a run-of-the mill chicken for a Poularde de Bresse.'

'A despot of the very worst kind,' said Jacques dryly. 'Stop at nothing.'

'That was the trouble.' Monsieur Pamplemousse rose to the Director's defence.

'When Monsieur Leclercq said he was reporting him he drew a knife…'

'*Touch*é,' said Jacques. 'And after he came out of prison, didn't he make a play for your Madame Grante before he got nabbed?'

'That's the one. It would be interesting to know if he is still inside.'

While they were talking, Pommes Frites drifted out to the kitchen, picked up his blanket, and carried it off to another room, curling up on the floor at the foot of his master's bed. If he was going to be on guard duty, he might as well be comfortable.

Shortly afterwards, Monsieur Pamplemousse followed on behind and, without even bothering to undress, closed the door behind him, turned off the light and lay back with his eyes closed, trying to marshal his thoughts into some kind of order.

The Director's situation was clear enough, but he found himself wondering how Madame Grante fitted into it all, or himself and Pommes Frites, come to that. Clearly if it were Dubois's handiwork, he wanted all three of them out of the way. The threats to Jo Jo, the attempt to discredit himself and Pommes Frites, bore the hallmarks of long-term planning. Talking to Jacques had set him wondering if *Le Guide*'s Head of Accounts still had a picture of Dubois by her bedside. More than likely she had thrown it away long ago, but you never knew.

So much had happened over the past few days it was like trying to assemble a giant jigsaw puzzle against the clock. His eyelids grew heavy, and before he was aware of what was happening, he fell into a dream concerning the proposed tasting.

It was taking place in the Director's office, and it involved a group of his closest friends and their pets, all of whom, including the dogs, were dressed for the occasion.

Towering above the competition, Pommes Frites seemed to have got it into his head that he was being tested on what *not* to eat. Blindfolded, he sank his teeth into what he clearly thought was a piece of sub-standard meat and, having discovered it was a dachshund, quickly spat it out. The victim gave a loud howl as it shot across the room, rebounded off a Chihuahua groping its way across Monsieur Leclercq's desk, and landed face down in a waste bin.

Understandably frightened out of its wits, the Chihuahua leapt onto Monsieur Leclercq's chair, where it relieved itself in no uncertain manner. Meanwhile, an Irish terrier, not wishing to be left out of things, deposited a sizeable *bronze* on the carpet.

To cap it all, an immaculately clad miniature Italian greyhound, having blundered into the offering while trying to escape, was so upset it elicited screams from all around as it began looking for something suitable against which it could wipe itself clean.

Above the hubbub he could hear Monsieur Leclercq's voice shouting his name: 'Pamplemousse! Pamplemousse, where are you?'

But by then he was too far away to answer, let alone care.

Having spotted Pommes Frites shedding his blindfold and making a bolt for it, he found himself careering after him on a bicycle.

Approaching a particularly steep section of a mountain road, Pommes Frites cleared it with a single bound, disappearing into a bank of low cloud.

Monsieur Pamplemousse was less fortunate. His bicycle having developed a squeak, the pedals became harder and harder to turn. His feet grew heavier and heavier with the effort, almost as though they were made of lead. And as the squeak turned into a groan, so the clouds got darker and darker, until they threatened to engulf him...

He tried brushing them aside, but they refused to move, and the more he tried the harder it became...until...he gave one last heave and woke to find he was clutching one of Pommes Frites' paws.

Almost immediately, he heard the familiar sound of his key finder. It seemed to be coming from another room...

Struggling into a sitting position and forcing himself awake, his first thought was to reach for the light switch, but smelling gas and realising the slightest spark could cause an explosion, he felt for his torch instead.

Undoing the bedroom door, he rushed into the kitchen and shone the light towards the stove. Registering the oven door was open, he hastily turned off the tap and made a dive for the window.

Pommes Frites joined him, and together they took a deep breath. Never had a draught of cold air felt so welcome.

A quick search of the rest of the apartment proved fruitless, and the hallway outside their apartment was in darkness. A single sweep with the torch showed the bulb from the overhead light had been removed.

Nose down, Pommes Frites made his way towards the lift. It was a forlorn hope, but Monsieur Pamplemousse pressed the down button, stifling his impatience as it seemed to take for ever to arrive.

As he feared, the trail petered out not far from their apartment block, suggesting that whoever the intruder was, he or she had used a car.

Returning to the living room, he automatically glanced up at the wall clock. Expecting it to show two, or perhaps even three o'clock, he was surprised to see it was still only a few minutes after eleven.

Checking through his list of dialling codes, he reached for the phone.

It was a long call and he had no sooner replaced the receiver than there was an incoming one.

'If I didn't know you better,' said Jacques, 'I would say you were trying to avoid me.'

'I was phoning Sicily,' said Monsieur Pamplemousse. 'Monsieur Leclercq's wife has an uncle there...'

'So I have heard tell.'

'I thought it was time he was brought up to date.'

'There are some things I would rather not know,' said Jacques unhappily.

'It might be as well if you did,' said Monsieur Pamplemousse.

As succinctly as possible, he spelt out what had happened. 'If it hadn't been for Pommes Frites keeping guard I might not be here now.

'I gave Chantal's uncle your number,' he continued,

breaking the silence, 'in case anything untoward happens. Uncle Caputo doesn't waste time once he has his mind set on something, and there could be other things you would rather not know about.'

'Thanks a heap,' said Jacques. 'Don't think I'm ungrateful, but the only reason I rang was to let you know Dubois came out of prison six months ago. Good behaviour, so they say.'

'It is all relative,' said Monsieur Pamplemousse.

'You should know,' said Jacques. He hesitated. 'Joking aside, I'm glad you're all right, Aristide.'

'I have Pommes Frites to thank for that,' said Monsieur Pamplemousse. 'Some of his presents come in very useful at times.'

CHAPTER TEN

Had Monsieur Pamplemousse been called upon to describe the scene in *Le Guide*'s fourth-floor boardroom the following morning, he would have been hard put to find the right words without resorting to his thesaurus. Even then, it certainly wouldn't have come under the sub-heading of TASTE: meaning flavour, gusto, palate, relish or savour, but rather UNSAVOURINESS, and all that went with it: loathsome, nauseous, repulsion and sickening.

The reason was all too apparent. Apart from Pommes Frites, those taking part in the tasting were of a vastly different calibre to the ones in his dream.

A more motley collection of cross-bred canines of doubtful parentage would have been hard to picture. Where they had all come from was anybody's guess. Straining and slobbering at their leashes, most looked as though they were more used to feeding out of dustbins rather than the Limoges china bowls provided by *Le Guide*'s catering staff.

Each and every one appeared more than ready to wolf down anything that was laid before it without so much as a second thought, let alone a preliminary sniff.

Monsieur Leclercq and his lawyers had certainly gone to town in preparing the ground to their best advantage.

Peace and quiet was in short supply, and the small but elite gathering of adjudicators seated on the sidelines looked as though they couldn't wait for the whole thing to be over.

He recognised several well-known names from the world of haute cuisine; among them Jay Corby, rotund food correspondent for a prominent American journal, who stood out from among a small group of well-known restaurant owners and their chefs, specially co-opted for the occasion.

Seated alongside them, although slightly apart, was a well-known judge; notorious for her short way with anyone who tested her patience, whether they were on the right side of the law or not.

Apart from Véronique, who was in charge of the tasting arrangements, she was the only female present. There was no sign of Maria.

The rest of the audience was made up of a small contingent from the fourth estate. Notebooks at the ready, they looked unsure as to why they were there at all.

At the appointed hour of 10 a.m. proceedings began with a dissertation by the renowned television pundit, animal expert and doyen of the canine show circuit, Oscar Durand.

A patrician figure in English tweeds, he had difficulty in making himself heard as he soliloquised on the sensitivity of dogs, notably bloodhounds, to smells...pause for a meaningful nod in Pommes Frites' direction, followed by a further pause as his gesture met with sporadic clapping from the staff.

As Durand moved on to instancing particular case histories;

the unique ability of certain breeds to search out narcotics and explosives, and the fact that, given suitable olfactory training, they could detect practically anything, from truffles to bedbugs, and – a recent exciting development – cancer in human beings, Monsieur Pamplemousse's attention began to wander.

Anxious to get down to brass tacks, he wondered if he had done the right thing in giving Pommes Frites an extra helping of breakfast that morning. He had done so in order to take the edge off his appetite in case hunger got the better of his normal instinct to seek out the best.

His sense of smell certainly hadn't deserted him. When they arrived at *Le Guide*'s headquarters that morning, he had gone straight to work.

Although barely 7 a.m., the large double gates were thrown wide open and the inner courtyard was alive with vans coming and going. He couldn't help noticing that even in the somewhat mundane area of delivering food, there was a definite pecking order. Those bearing illustrious names in the world of *boucherie* metaphorically elbowed their way in front of others belonging to various *supermarchés*, as though it were a God-given right.

Canteen staff were already on duty helping to unload trays of meat; *Le Guide*'s resident chef, Claude Bouquet, armed with a clipboard, meticulously ticking off each new arrival. At its height, it could have been a miniature replica of Rungis market at dawn.

Ignoring all the commotion, Pommes Frites, nose to the ground, tail erect, made a bee-line for the gatekeeper's lodge. Unfazed by the fact that the door appeared to be locked, he took off in another direction, following a trail that led him first of all to the Smart car, still parked in the same place, then towards the main entrance. Only when he came up against the revolving doors did his tail begin to droop, presumably because the scent merged with too many others to separate it.

If nothing else, it confirmed in Monsieur Pamplemousse's mind the identity of the previous night's visitor. Thank goodness it hadn't been Doucette all on her own; although, having said that, given the time the break-in took place, the intruder must have been somewhere outside on the look-out for his and Pommes Frites' return.

If the present trail were fresh, it must mean Dubois was somewhere on the premises, perhaps involved in some way with the preparations, and he wondered what his reaction would be if and when he caught sight of them. It could bring matters to a head.

Suddenly realising Durand had stopped talking and the Director was about to hold forth, he tried to concentrate on the job in hand.

'The procedure is simple,' began Monsieur Leclercq. 'Each of the dogs taking part will be presented with three bowls. For the sake of clarity they will be marked A, B and C. The first round will involve cooked chicken, the second lamb and the third beef.

'On each occasion one of the bowls will contain a top-quality product from a premier supplier – a known specialist in that particular area. The other two bowls will contain a lower-grade meat. The object of the exercise is to ascertain the animals' reaction to being given a choice. Will they, *par exemple*, show any indication of singling out one as being preferable to the other two?

'We are leaving our own Pommes Frites until last, as the

object of the exercise is to demonstrate that he is a dog of taste and discernment and, after a preliminary inspection, will always, without any hesitation, choose the best.'

Monsieur Pamplemousse glanced at the clock on the wall. The thespian in Monsieur Leclercq was beginning to take over. Any moment now he would be back in his favourite role, that of Robespierre the Incorruptible.

In Monsieur Pamplemousse's humble opinion, anyone who believed the people of France should exist on a diet of lentils would have been a most unsuitable candidate for being Director of *Le Guide*.

Robespierre had undoubtedly been an orator *par excellence* but, like Monsieur Leclercq, once he was in full flow, had been hard to stop. In the end, he was only silenced by his own hand when he shot himself in the mouth rather than be shouted down.

Far be it for him to dwell on such parallels, but as the Director paused to make sure all the points had sunk in, Monsieur Pamplemousse couldn't help but feel proud of his use of the words 'our own' when referring to Pommes Frites.

In any case, his thoughts were interrupted by the Judge.

'May I,' she called, 'be permitted to ask if the prime product will always be in the same lettered bowl?'

'No, madame,' replied Monsieur Leclercq. 'The arrangement will be entirely at random. The only person to know the answer to that question will be my secretary.' He motioned towards Véronique. She will announce it before each sitting.

'How do we know your dog can't read?' asked a member of the press, eliciting giggles from the rest of the corps.

The Judge fixed the speaker with a freezing stare. Had he

been in the dock, the poor man would undoubtedly have been sentenced on the spot for contempt of court.

'I am sure Pommes Frites will happily submit to being blindfolded,' said Monsieur Leclercq hurriedly, 'although I hardly think that is necessary.

'For the benefit of those among us who have a vested interest in knowing where the prime products originate,' he continued, 'let me tell you the chicken is from Le Poulet de Bresse in the 16th *arrondissement*, the lamb is from Jean-Paul Gardil on the Ile St Louis – we are fortunate in that respect as the first of the season's *agneau des Pyrénées* has just arrived. The beef is from Boucherie Jean-Jacques, also in the 16th.'

There was a murmur of approval from the chefs, and pencils raced across pads as those in the press corps took their cue. Monsieur Pamplemousse couldn't help thinking it might be well worth eating in the canteen for the next few days, assuming there was any meat left over.

'And now, if the handlers will all move to the far end of the room,' said Monsieur Leclercq, 'we will arrange for the first dishes to be brought in.'

While this was happening, he moved across and joined Monsieur Pamplemousse.

'I trust Pommes Frites' taste buds are on song,' he hissed. 'A great deal rests on his shoulders.'

'I am quietly confident,' said Monsieur Pamplemousse. 'I don't think he has much to fear from the opposition, although I doubt if their owners will thank you. They have probably never had it so good. Future appetites will have been whetted.'

'The team assembling them excelled themselves,' said Monsieur Leclercq. 'As for the owners; people who allow their dogs to roam the streets of Paris in the early hours are asking for trouble. That said, I doubt if many of those here today can lay claim to having an owner. They are probably counting themselves fortunate to end up with a free meal in pleasant surroundings, the like of which they probably haven't experienced for a long time.

'Perhaps we should have blindfolded them after all,' he mused. 'They will probably be hanging around in the rue Fabert for weeks to come. I must issue instructions to Bourdel.'

'I didn't see him this morning,' ventured Monsieur Pamplemousse. 'Is he in today?'

'He volunteered to oversee security arrangements behind the scenes,' said Monsieur Leclercq. 'I have sent for Rambaud to help out. I hope he doesn't take too long getting here. He isn't always that quick off the mark and he is very set in his ways...' He broke off as Véronique entered with the first of the dishes on a tray.

Knowing how ponderous Rambaud could be when he felt like it, Monsieur Pamplemousse felt the Director was being a trifle overoptimistic and subsequent events proved him right.

Dog after dog obeyed Véronique's call, and without pausing for breath, devoured the entire contents of the bowls; nearest first, furthest away last. Licked cleaned until it would have been possible to see their faces in them, all but one dish survived the onslaught. The exception fell victim to a Rottweiler with yellowing teeth. Much to Chef Bouquet's evident disgust, it broke into several pieces. Worse still, when he tried to retrieve them, he narrowly escaped a mauling himself.

Monsieur Pamplemousse regretted not having armed

himself with a camera. There were Cartier-Bresson moments galore.

For his part, Pommes Frites viewed the goings-on with detached interest.

Why Monsieur Leclercq should be throwing a party, asking all manner of stray dogs along, was beyond his understanding. He would much sooner have had a quiet meal with his master somewhere; just the two of them. On the other hand, there was no accounting for the way human beings behaved at times, and it was usually best to humour them. If the Director wanted to give him an early lunch, then so be it. He wasn't complaining.

He pricked up his ears as Monsieur Leclercq began speaking again.

'There are no prizes,' he said, 'for guessing which chicken will prove the best of the three. Bresse is the only poultry in the world to enjoy the protection of a controlled name: *Appellation d'Origine Controllée.* To acquire that accolade they have to meet strict criteria, not only in their breeding, but in the presentation. As the great French gastronome Brillat-Savarin once put it: "When fattened, the birds of Bresse are to cuisine what canvas is to painters, or the cap of Fortunatus to charlatans."

'All three birds have been cooked to perfection by Chef Bouquet. All that remains is for Pommes Frites to choose which, in his considered opinion, is the best.'

Resting his case, the Director signalled Monsieur Pamplemousse to release his charge.

'It is in bowl B,' said Véronique, breaking the hush that came over the audience.

Instinctively sensing what was required of him, Pommes

Frites made a show of giving all three bowls a preliminary sniff, then made light work of the chicken in the middle one.

A round of applause went up as he returned to Monsieur Pamplemousse, licking his lips.

He was beginning to enjoy himself. Travelling the length and breadth of France with his master, he had been lucky enough to encounter a great many excellent meals over the years, but never before had he been applauded for eating one.

In the short time at his disposal he had worked out in his own mind what was happening. All the other dogs were there to be auditioned for his post. If that were the case, he would show them. Spurred on by his success, he couldn't wait for the arrival of the next course.

'This test, involving the lamb,' announced the Director, 'is a good deal harder. Apart from *agneau de lait des Pyrénées...*'

'Which is in bowl C,' Véronique broke in on cue.

'...we have also included a *pré-salé* lamb from Normandy, which, as I am sure you all know, is famous for the very special taste imparted by virtue of the sheep having grazed on the iodine-rich flora of coastal pasturelands when the tide is out. However, in my opinion, it doesn't hold a candle to lambs born from sheep that have spent the summer months grazing on the grassy slopes of the Pyrénées, rich in all manner of wild flowers and herbs. That, too, is a very special taste.'

Monsieur Pamplemousse felt a momentary unease, wondering if his friend and mentor would take one sniff and compare Chef Bouquet's handiwork unfavourably with Martine's.

But he needn't have worried. Having clearly awarded the *pré-salé* lamb second place, Pommes Frites chose the one from the Pyrénées. This time he waited for the applause to die down before returning to his master.

Pencils in the hands of the press corps literally flew across their pads.

'No photographs, please,' said Monsieur Leclercq, as a member of the group held up a camera. 'I have my reasons,' he added. 'We do not seek publicity at this stage.'

'And now, we come to perhaps the sternest test of all: beef.

'Many people would nominate Charolais as being the best in all France.'

'Bowl A,' chimed in Veronique.

'Again, as the chefs among you will know, Charolais cattle bear a Label Rouge, which means they have been raised on a diet of at least three parts grass to one part grain, and have spent around ten months outdoors.

'By law, the meat must be dry-aged for a minimum of eight days in a refrigerated room at just above freezing; ideally, for anything up to three weeks.

'As with all the prime products being used in these tests, when the time comes to transport the animals for slaughter, it must be carried out humanely and without any stress, which would impair the quality. The carcasses must also be guaranteed free of growth hormones and antibiotics.

'However, in the opinion of many gourmets, the best beef of all comes not from from Burgundy, but from Aubrac in the Auvergne...'

As Pommes Frites made his way forward Véronique, finger to her lips, nodded towards bowl B.

Monsieur Pamplemousse breathed a sigh of relief. It was his home territory, and he knew Pommes Frites shared his tastes.

'Once again,' continued the Director, 'it is a matter of what the animals feed on in the wild. The heights of the Auvergne, over one thousand metres above sea level, are rich in herbs, gentian and the like, which imparts a wonderful taste to the naturally marbled meat.'

It was a controversial statement, which was immediately taken up by some members of the assembly.

Jay Corby began extolling the virtues of American beef. 'The reason why it's the best in the world is because the cattle are killed off at a much earlier age – eighteen months; then we age it longer.'

'If I tell you Aubrac is the first choice of Michel Bras, who for many years has enjoyed three Stock Pots in *Le Guide*,' persisted Monsieur Leclercq, 'I feel that says it all...'

The Judge held up her hand again. 'If Aubrac beef is so good,' she said, 'why is your dog refusing to go anywhere near it?'

'What?' Monsieur Leclercq broke off in mid-flight.

He stared round the room, seeking help first of all from Véronique, who shook her head, clearly at a loss as to what had gone wrong, then at Monsieur Pamplemousse.

'Perhaps,' said Monsieur Pamplemousse, 'with all due respect to those behind the scenes, the bowls have become transposed.'

'I hardly think that can be the case,' said the Judge. 'He is also refusing to touch bowl A. Yet, albeit reluctantly, he has finished off what you choose to call a lesser product from a *supermarché*. Clearly, he is of the opinion that is the best.'

A chorus of agreement rose from those around her.

For once, even the Director was temporarily at a loss for words.

Attention focused on Monsieur Pamplemousse as Pommes Frites raced out of the room. Leaping to his feet he pointed to the bowls. 'Nobody,' he ordered, 'but *nobody* touch them while I am gone!'

Reliving his dream, he tore out of the room in hot pursuit of Pommes Frites. Only this time, instead of chasing after him on a bicycle, he headed towards the ground floor, taking the stairs two at a time.

He could tell by the set of the ears, the angle of the tail, the rate at which he was travelling as he left the boardroom, Pommes Frites was in deadly earnest about something. Speed was of the essence.

But he was too late. Arriving in the courtyard via the Director's private entrance, he realised the Smart car was no longer there. Neither was Pommes Frites. He carried on into the street, but there was still no sign of either.

It was some while before Monsieur Pamplemousse returned to the fourth floor, practically on his knees after a fruitless search of the area. The boardroom was empty of visitors; the long table, the chairs and other furnishings back in place.

To his intense joy Pommes Frites was waiting for him, looking none the worse for wherever it was he had been, but clearly suffering mixed feelings. Greetings over, he drew his master's attention to a note on the table. It was from the Director, requesting their presence in his office.

'There you are, Pamplemousse!' boomed Monsieur Leclercq as they entered. 'I was beginning to fear the worst. You will have heard the news, of course. Bourdel must have suffered some kind of mental breakdown. Apparently he came rushing out of the building like a being possessed, jumped into that wretched Smart car of his and shot off at an incredible speed. The whole thing was extraordinary.

'Those who witnessed it could scarcely believe their eyes. For some reason he seemed unable to stop. Wrestling with the steering wheel, he went twice round the fountain before shooting out into the rue Fabert.

'Fortunately the gates were still wide open, otherwise they would have suffered untold damage. As it was, he only just managed to turn left without overturning before heading towards the Seine with Pommes Frites hard on his heels. Have you any idea what it all means?'

'I suspect,' said Monsieur Pamplemousse, 'the answer is much like those phrases one learnt by rote as a small child during English lessons. The one I particularly remember is: "the lady who is opening the window is my aunt." In all my years I have never had occasion to use it. In fact, I am not sure I have ever seen any of my aunts open a window, even in the height of summer. The Auvergnat are wary of making rash decisions.'

The Director stared at him. 'Don't tell me you have an aunt involved in all of this, Pamplemousse. Why was I not informed?'

Monsieur Pamplemousse mentally counted up to ten. 'In this particular case, monsieur,' he said, 'for "aunt" you need to substitute the word "uncle".

'The phrase I have in mind would be along the lines of: "*L'homme qui pouvrait réprondre á la question est l'oncle de ma femme.*" The literal English translation being: "The man who could answer the question is my wife's uncle."'

'Doucette?'

'No, monsieur...' Manfully, Monsieur Pamplemousse avoided saying 'try again'. 'I am referring to Madame Leclercq...'

The Director stared at him as light slowly dawned.

'Chantal. You mean…Chantal's Uncle Caputo?'

'*Exactement!* I think, monsieur, your troubles are over.'

Monsieur Leclercq crossed to his cocktail cabinet. The Roullet Très Hors Age had been replaced by a bottle of Gosset Grande Réserve Champagne. Removing it from the ice bucket, he carefully poured two glasses.

'Four hundred years in one family,' he said. 'Continuity, Aristide; that is what France is all about. I had Véronique prepare it in readiness to celebrate Pommes Frites' victory in the tasting, which I had assumed to be a foregone conclusion. But if what you say is true, it is splendid news. Even more cause for celebration.'

He raised his glass.

'I don't know how you do it, Pamplemousse.'

'Sometimes,' said Monsieur Pamplemousse. 'I wonder myself, although in this particular instance it is Uncle Caputo you should thank. My part was very minor.'

Thinking it over while he had been looking for Pommes Frites, he realised it was little wonder Dubois had plotted to get Madame Grante out of the way, along with anyone else who might remember him from his previous attempt to sabotage *Le Guide*; namely himself and Pommes Frites, who had literally sunk his teeth into him when he had tried to escape.

'Dubois wanted to satisfy himself that I wasn't a danger,' he said. 'To that end he acquired the photographs of me feeding Pommes Frites. At the same time he started sending threatening notes to Madame Grante, thus effectively removing the three most dangerous elements in his plan.

'Strangely enough, although I was instrumental in having him sent away the last time, we never actually met face to face. I only knew him from a photograph Madame Grante had in her apartment. She was very smitten at the time.'

'I do remember that,' said the Director. 'Poor lady. Hell hath no fury like a woman scorned.'

'The only exception,' said Monsieur Pamplemousse, 'is a woman whose pet budgerigar has been threatened with a fate worse than death.

'Once she was gone it left the way clear for Maria to insist you get rid of Rambaud, and that in turn left the door open for Dubois to move in. I imagine when we open up the gatekeeper's lodge we shall find a lot of interesting pieces of equipment.'

'It all sounds immensely complicated.'

'Complicated, and yet remarkably simple,' said Monsieur Pamplemousse. 'During the time Dubois was in prison the idea must have taken root in his mind and begun to grow like a cancer.

'Revenge is sweet, and there are all manner of other ways he could have brought it about. But having tried once and failed, he wanted to make absolutely certain it would work this time, with the added bonus of his being on the spot to witness this whole edifice collapse, taking everyone with it.

'I suspect that when the beef is examined, you will find it contains poison. It must have been a desperate last move on his part, and when that failed he knew the game was up.'

Monsieur Leclercq opened a desk drawer. 'I gather from Véronique that you have lost your watch, Aristide. I trust you will accept this replacement as a small token of my, and indeed *Le Guide*'s, gratitude and appreciation.

'I fear it is not of French origin. Cupillard Rième are no longer with us; a sign of the times, if you will excuse the pun.

It is manufactured in Switzerland by a company called Jean d'Eve, but I am assured it keeps excellent time nonetheless.

'It is a pity Véronique isn't here to join in the celebration,' he continued, waving aside Monsieur Pamplemousse's thanks. 'She asked if she could leave early. Something to do with being locked out of her own apartment on account of forgetting a password. I couldn't make head nor tail of it.'

As they left the building, Monsieur Pamplemousse was in the act of pocketing the watch case when he felt a familiar shape and realised his Cross pen had been there all the time. It must have slipped down inside the lining.

All of a sudden, everything seemed right with the world again. Taking out his mobile, he rang Doucette to tell her the coast was clear.

'You may be back before me,' he said. 'I have to visit Véronique first. It sounds as though she needs me. She is unable to enter her apartment.'

'A locksmith…?

'No, Couscous, it is more complicated than that. It has to do with champagne glasses being taller this year.

'I will explain when I see you.'

Jacques rested his knife and fork and sat back. 'I used to think,' he said, 'that as one grew older things would start to slow down, but the reverse is true. Whatever happened to November?'

'Pommes Frites and I went back to the Auvergne,' said Monsieur Pamplemousse. 'Sadly, we missed out on Michel Bras. He was already closed for the winter.'

'And December?'

'Much the same. Except we spent Christmas with Doucette's sister. No turkey, I'm afraid.'

'Don't tell me,' said Jacques.

Monsieur Pamplemousse nodded. 'Agathe tried a new version of it this time. She served *tripes à la mode de Caen* with jelly made from sparkling Cerdon wine and cranberries.'

'And?'

'*Désastre!* She burnt the jelly, would you believe?'

'That can't have been easy.'

'Difficult, but clearly not impossible.'

'Talking of disasters,' said Jacques, 'you know we found Dubois's car...'

'I read something about it,' said Monsieur Pamplemousse. 'I gather the wreckage was in a wood near Melun. Paradoxically, that is where my sister-in-law lives.'

'It's a small world.'

'Burnt out, I gather. No trace of the driver. It didn't say any more.'

'What's one burnt-out car these days?' said Jacques. 'It isn't news any more.'

'Putting the pieces together again, the boffins found the brakes had been disconnected and the accelerator pedal tampered with so that it jammed down. I can't imagine who would have done a thing like that, can you?'

Monsieur Pamplemousse shook his head.

'It must have been one hell of a drive.'

'Horrendous,' said Monsieur Pamplemousse, 'but on the other hand, an extraordinary feat.'

'He committed over three hundred and fifty traffic offences on the way,' said Jacques. 'Ignoring red lights, travelling the wrong way down one-way streets, you name it. If the extradition order is granted, which I very much doubt will happen; we will throw the book at him.'

Monsieur Pamplemousse paused over his soufflé Grand Marnier.

'You know where he is?'

'Your boss's wife's Uncle Caputo has taken him on as his personal driver,' said Jacques. 'A bit ironical since he set out to eliminate him. But, as you once told me, he knows quality when he sees it. I can't see Dubois ever bothering *Le Guide* again. It would be more than his life is worth. As it is, I gather his hair turned white overnight.'

They ate in silence for a moment or two while Monsieur Pamplemousse digested the information.

'While you've been away,' said Jacques, 'I have been looking up pesticides. According to the analyst, that stuff Dubois injected into Pommes Frites' meat was aldrin; it's one of a group used against used against infestation by flies and mosquitoes… wireworms, caterpillars, that kind of thing.

'It's been banned in many parts of the world, but apparently your old gatekeeper has been using it for years; something to do with having caterpillars in his window box. He was grumbling like mad that someone had been at the packet.'

'I can picture it,' said Monsieur Pamplemousse. 'Rambaud's window box is his pride and joy.'

'Taken by humans or other animals, aldrin causes dizziness, vomiting, convulsions, respiratory failure. It would have been a nasty way to go.

'What bothers me, is according to my information, it is completely odourless, so…'

'…what made Pommes Frites reject the meat?'

'Exactly.'

'Bloodhounds are good at putting two and two together,' said Monsieur Pamplemousse. 'My guess is he must have smelt the person who tampered with it. And that person had to be Dubois. He smelt a rat in more ways than one.'

'Sorry I asked,' said Jacques.

'For a brief while, Pommes Frites' future hung in the balance; mine too. But when it was discovered how much poison had been injected into the beef everyone changed their tune.'

'A useful *camarade* to have about the house.' Jacques gazed down at the recumbent form under the table.

'He saved my life,' said Monsieur Pamplemousse simply.

'That too,' said Jacques. 'I wonder what he would have done if he'd been human?'

'Changed his butcher, I expect,' said Monsieur Pamplemousse. 'Pommes Frites has a refreshingly uncomplicated approach to life. He sees things strictly in terms of black and white; right and wrong.'

'As for Maria,' said Jacques. 'She seems to have disappeared off the face of the earth. I take it you have heard nothing more from her?'

'Well, yes and no,' said Monsieur Pamplemousse.

Jacques downed his wine. 'Come on, Aristide...out with it. Between friends and these four walls...'

By way of an answer, Monsieur Pamplemousse removed a small package from his pocket and placed it on the table.

'Going back to Christmas,' he said, 'just before Twelfth Night, a parcel containing a small cake arrived at Monsieur Leclercq's office.'

'*Galette de Roi!*' Jacques made a face. 'I know it's traditional, but I can't stand frangipane and it's usually full of it. As for those little statue things people put inside them – I once nearly broke a tooth on one.'

'*Fèves*,' said Monsieur Pamplemousse. 'I thought they were always slipped into the cake somewhere near the edge so that wouldn't happen.'

'So did I,' said Jacques ruefully. 'Blame the wife. Things weren't too good back at the works in those days. Don't say you've brought me a slice.'

'Again, it's a case of yes and no.'

Unwrapping the parcel, Monsieur Pamplemousse revealed the end of a tie. Inside it was a small porcelain figurine.

'Monsieur Leclercq has entrusted me with this for the time being. He doesn't want it left lying around in case it gets into the wrong hands. Madame Leclercq's, *par exemple*.'

Jacques examined the object. 'I can't say I blame him.' Lowering his voice, he looked around to make sure no one else was watching. 'I don't know about the girl who's dressed up as a nun – she looks a pretty little thing, but the guy fumbling with her zip is the spitting image of your boss. I've seen porno *fèves* advertised on a website – Kama Sutra pigs…rabbits…that kind of thing, but this one beats them all. It looks as though it must have been specially made.'

'Whoever sent it probably had a lot of photo references to help them,' said Monsieur Pamplemousse.

'The parcel was postmarked Sicily. I strongly suspect Uncle Caputo has taken Maria on board as well. As I said earlier, he respects genuine talent when he sees it and he hates letting it go to waste.'

'Our loss could be Sicily's gain…' said Jacques.

'It is what Monsieur Leclercq calls an elegant solution.'

'That depends where you are sitting,' said Jacques.

'Elegant, but hardly kosher. All the same, it saves on paper-work...'

'Lawyer's fees too,' said Monsieur Pamplemousse. 'At the end of the day, they are the only ones who grow fat out of other people's misfortunes.'

Jacques pushed his chair way from the table. 'Thanks for the meal. Some of us have to get back to work.'

'All good things...' said Monsieur Pamplemousse. 'As for this restaurant. It doesn't know yet, so don't breathe a word, but they are in line to receive a Stock Pot. This meal was by way of a final check-up, courtesy of *Le Guide*.'

'I thought you said it was your treat.'

'I didn't say I was paying. I simply said you could choose the restaurant, and the wine, of course. Incidentally, I admire your choice: Beaune Clos de Roi from Tollot-Beaut was a perfect accompaniment to the *boeuf en croute*.'

'You don't want an assistant with a talent for this kind of thing, do you?' asked Jacques. 'Clean-living, able to carry your bags, grovel when required, fond of travel, not frightened of long hours...'

'If you hear of anyone like that,' said Monsieur Pamplemousse, 'give me a ring. And thank you again for all your help. Keep the *fève* – you can change it for a free copy of *Le Guide* when it comes out.'

Calling for the bill, he waited until they were out in the street before reaching for his mobile. There was one other important call he had to make.

'Congratulations,' said Mr Pickering when he had finished. 'Most satisfactory. But if you don't mind my saying so, it does sound a very French solution.'

'With Italian overtones,' said Monsieur Pamplemousse. 'Let

us not forget that. One should always give credit where credit is due.'

Glancing down as he said goodbye, he could have sworn Pommes Frites was smiling to himself, but then, he often did at the end of a case.